ISLAND GIRL

The Curse of the Evil Tattoo

PATRICIA DISTAD

with Illustrations by Dodge Distad
and Cover by Kay Zetlmaier

authorHOUSE®

AuthorHouse™
1663 Liberty Drive
Bloomington, IN 47403
www.authorhouse.com
Phone: 1 (800) 839-8640

Published by AuthorHouse   09/23/2015

ISBN: 978-1-5049-2041-4 (sc)
ISBN: 978-1-5049-2040-7 (e)

Library of Congress Control Number: 2015910868

Print information available on the last page.

After her father's untimely death, Sawyer and her mother moved to her grandparent's farm in Kansas. Now 5 years later she faces some important challenges when her mother attends a reunion and reconnects with her high school sweetheart, Major Bradley Sommers.

Their marriage creates a new blended family including Bradley's son Grady. Sawyer's life is put in turmoil when they leave her grandparent's farm to follow Bradley to his new duty station in Hawaii. Life becomes even more complicated when Grady arrives from his high school graduation road trip with a strange tattoo.

Plagued by nightmares and the disapproval of his father, Grady turns to Sawyer for help. Together they embark on a journey filled with risks, dangerous rescues, and unexpected love.

For my granddaughters
Maizie and Piper

ACKNOWLEDGEMENTS

I want to thank the many people who supported me with their expertise and friendship: Fran Berman, Pat Nelson, Erik Nelson, Dane Henriksen, Adrienne Reeves, Connie Halpren, my ever supportive husband John, and my family. A special thanks to my son Dodge who challenged me to make this novel as authentic as possible and to my granddaughters, Maizie and Piper, who wanted me to tell them a story and make it into a "real book."

I could not have written a novel rich in detail without my editor Josh Grapes. During the long process of editing he taught me how to write. Thank you for your patience, inspiring comments, and making it so much fun.

The settings in the book are based upon those I have seen during my trips to Hawaii. Though the characters share many traits and experiences with people I know, this is a work of fiction.

TABLE OF CONTENTS

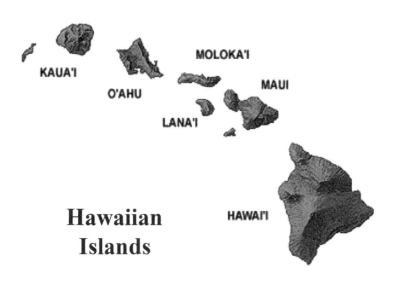

Hawaiian Islands

KAUA'I

O'AHU

MOLOKA'I

LANA'I

MAUI

HAWAI'I

Oahu

CHAPTER 1

The Wedding

"This can't be happening," Sawyer thought to herself for the umpteenth time. She stood beside her mother and watched her adjust her bridal gown in the full-length mirror. Julie's hands slid down to straighten her skirt, then met her daughter's eyes reflected in the mirror. A rush of love, uncertainty, and guilt overwhelmed her.

The wedding ceremony was about to begin. Julie put her arm around Sawyer and tried to reassure her.

"I know you're upset about moving, but this will be a great adventure. You know how much we both mean to Bradley and Grady."

Tears slid down Sawyer's face. "I know Mom," she whispered. "It's just so hard to leave home, especially Papa and Gran."

"We've talked about this, honey, and we decided we could do it. They're happy for us and they'll come visit at Christmas. By then you'll be able to give them quite a tour." Julie squeezed Sawyer's hand. "Now, are you ready to be my maid of honor?"

Sawyer drew in a deep breath and nodded. She tucked her unruly blonde hair behind her ear and glanced down at the pantyhose drooping at her knees and tried again to get the bunched-up hose stretched tight from her ankles up to her waist. She was surprised she liked her dress. Her mom let her pick it out. It wasn't fussy with too much lace or ruffles, but it had a scooped neckline and capped sleeves. It flowed over Sawyer's skinny body, ending right at her knees. Sawyer never thought her mom would allow her to wear red at the wedding. Though her mother grimaced at the notion, she eventually gave in to the brilliant color. Sawyer failed to persuade her to let her wear tennis shoes instead of the tight, painful stacked heels, dyed red to match her dress. Sawyer was a jock. She only owned tennis shoes, running shoes, and soccer shoes. These were her first heels and her only dress. "This is just the beginning," Mom said. "One day you'll love wearing dresses and heels."

As if turning 12 was a magical step between being a kid and becoming a young lady! Sawyer thought as she nodded out of respect. She couldn't imagine ever choosing a dress over her jeans and her dad's old red basketball jersey.

The music drifted in. It was time. They walked together to the entrance of the chapel where Papa stood waiting. He was every bit the gentleman in his dark suit and bow tie. He picked out the blue one with gold horseshoes on it. He said it was his good luck tie, perfect for this momentous day. The tie was a bit crooked as usual. It made Sawyer giggly and sad at the same time. She reached up to straighten it for him and wondered if Gran would take over this chore when she moved away. The look on his face almost made her give in to tears again, but instead she gave him a brave smile. He held up his hand for a high five. She slapped it, turned, and strode down the aisle, clutching a bouquet of sunflowers and trying not to stumble.

When she reached the altar, she glanced at the groom, Major Bradley Sommers, and his son and best man Grady. They nodded and smiled at each other, though each was experiencing mixed emotions. Bradley stood at attention, every bit the Marine, with his piercing blue eyes and his black hair cut as though he was ready for an inspection. Grady fidgeted, shifting his lanky frame from side to side. Even at 17, he was unsure how to act. Sawyer turned to face her family and their guests. She watched her mother come down the aisle on Papa's arm. Her mom made a beautiful bride. Her hazel eyes sparkled as she walked with grace and apparent confidence, though she gripped her father's arm a little too tightly. She wore a simple ivory silk sheath that fell to her ankles. Instead of a veil, her blonde hair was pulled into a French twist with Gran's antique comb holding it in place. A few strands escaped and curled at her chin.

Her smile radiated, but Sawyer thought she could detect her eyes fluttering a little too rapidly. She knew this meant her mom was not as calm as she'd like everyone to think.

Sawyer returned her mother's smile and gave her special, private wink. In spite of it all, she wanted her mom to be happy today, not to focus on the turmoil this wedding was causing the whole family. It had been five years since her father was killed in a car accident. He'd tried to avoid a boy on a bicycle who'd wandered out into his lane. The boy was fine, but her father crashed into a brick pillar and didn't make it. When the police came to the house and told them what had happened, Sawyer and her mom were devastated. They took turns falling apart and trying to comfort each other. They huddled together on Sawyer's bed, ignoring the ringing phone and chiming doorbell, the sound of neighbors and friends interrupting grief with good intentions. Gran would tiptoe in and put plates of fruit, peanut-buttered toast, and lemonade on the bedside table. It was days before the two of them emerged from their shared isolation to face the world.

Julie had always stayed at home with Sawyer, so there was no income to support them. Papa and Gran offered to bring them home to Kansas and they gratefully accepted. Her grandparents had an old farmhouse on the outskirts of Colby, a small town just over the Colorado border. Sawyer made good friends over the last five years, excelled in track and soccer, planted vegetable gardens with Papa, and learned to cook family recipes with Gran. She even raised a pig as a 4H project and shed a few tears when Bacon Bits was sold at the county fair.

Julie worked as the director of the Heartland Museum and loved all the historical projects that made the site special. She'd just arranged to move a 19th century barn to the property to use for events, but the life they'd built so painstakingly changed when Julie reconnected with her old sweetheart at the Colby High School Reunion. Bradley had come home on leave to visit his parents while Grady spent a few weeks with his mother. They were surprised to run into each other that night.

Sawyer was amazed when her mother showed a spark of interest at Bradley's attention. He kept calling her and making trips to see them, and the budding relationship became serious. Sawyer was happy for her mother. Though he'd never be a father to Sawyer, she was certain Bradley truly cared about both of them.

Sawyer turned her head for another peek at Bradley, so handsome in his uniform. She was touched by his look of pride and love as he took her mother's hand from Papa, who gave his daughter a quick teary-eyed kiss and joined Gran in the first row. She remembered the day she realized that her mother was going to marry Bradley, that they'd have to leave everything behind to follow him to his next duty station. After that, Sawyer spent many evenings rocking back and forth on the porch swing, sharing her doubts and fears with Gran and Papa. No matter how hard they tried, there just wasn't a solution that suited everyone.

Sawyer glanced over to Grady. He was still shuffling from one foot to another. She didn't mind him either. He was nice to her most of the time. She never had a brother or a sister before, so a new big brother was a definite bonus. He was tall and skinny with sandy hair he never combed. She liked the way his grey eyes twinkled when he was tickled about something. He loved to give her a hard time, and he'd tease her until her cheeks went hot and red, but Sawyer knew that Grady liked her. Just before the ceremony, he rested his hand on her shoulder and said, "Everything will be okay, Slick. You'll see."

Sawyer's eyes moved to her grandparents, sitting hand-in-hand, smiling at her with a look of resignation. She knew they wanted to be supportive, but their hearts were broken, and now here they were at the chapel, dabbing at their eyes so their tears wouldn't spoil the moment. They tried not to think about the ceremony, the vows, the reception – all the final steps before their precious daughter and granddaughter would leave them.

"You may now kiss the bride," the minister said.

Julie smiled at Bradley, but her stomach was still tied up. She hoped her happiness didn't come at too great a cost. Would Bradley's love be enough to make up for the loss of their Kansas home? It was a lot to ask. Julie worried about Bradley too. He was taking on a new wife and daughter at a crucial point in his career. The uncertainty of the military lifestyle had kept her sleepless for the last few nights, but in spite of her concerns, Julie believed in their love. She was ready to marry this remarkable man and become a military wife.

The kiss itself was short and respectful. The minister let them savor the moment, and then announced, "May I present Major and Mrs. Bradley Sommers."

The guests clapped and smiled. Some even whistled or shouted their approval. With all the energy in the air, even Grady couldn't help but crack a smile. Sawyer swore she wasn't going to cry, but a jumble of emotions got the better of her. This moment would change their lives forever. Mom and Bradley turned to Sawyer.

Bradley wiped a tear from her cheek and her mom kissed her. Mom wrapped her arms around her new stepson and gave him a light pat on the back. Bradley shook his son's damp hand with a firm grip.

Then, at last, they went down the aisle as a family.

CHAPTER 2

Goodbye

It's a good thing the wedding was yesterday! Sawyer thought. Spring in Kansas meant anything could happen. Yesterday was warm and calm, but today the clouds blew flurries. The ground was covered by a thin layer of snow. Sawyer's tennis shoes made a crunching sound as she hauled her backpack to the car. The snow would melt by noon, but it made their departure even harder.

Grady was up early packing his duffle bag and his backpack. His friend Vic was picking him up at the Colorado border for what they called "The Great Escape." Grady was taking a road trip to California as his graduation present. He'd catch up to his new family after a month of adventure. He hadn't decided if his next step was college, work, or the Marines. Even Bradley wasn't sure what was right for his son.

Grady wasn't a great student. In fact, he barely squeaked by. It had been difficult for him to move from one duty station to another. Making good friends and fitting into new schools with challenging academic expectations kept him off balance. He never knew where he stood with the teachers, his classmates, or especially his father. He didn't even know how much he meant to his mother. Grady was hurt and angry with her after the divorce. She gave him lots of "good reasons" for leaving him behind with his father, but Grady couldn't help but feel she just didn't want him getting in the way of her new life. He took out his disappointment on his father. He'd resisted their last move to Washington D.C., rebelled at school, ditched classes, didn't bother with assignments, and made his father's life miserable. Bradley was so relieved his son had graduated, even if it was with a D average, that he choked up at the ceremony.

"We'll call as soon as we get there," Julie assured her parents.

"I'll send the wedding proofs when we get them, sweetie," Gran said, with a catch in her voice.

Grady stood by the packed car. He felt for Sawyer. He remembered his many departures and the emptiness that followed. He envied the love her family displayed so openly. Desperate hugs and tears prevailed until Bradley said, "We better get going. It may take longer to get to Colorado Springs with the snow, and we don't want to miss our flight."

Sawyer climbed in the backseat with Grady and squeezed her bear, Gaboochie, hoping his soft furry body would help her over the next few minutes. Papa gave her the bear after her father died. He told her to hug him whenever she was sad or lonesome and she'd feel a little better. Gaboochie had curly white fur, big brown eyes and a soft black leather nose. His perky ears stood up straight and his mouth curved into a wistful smile. After five years of cuddling, he was a bit dingy. Gran's Irish Setter Clancy had chewed on his nose and made it scratchy. The stuffing settled into his right leg so he

could no longer sit upright, but Sawyer didn't care. He smelled like home and she was grateful to have him to hold against her breaking heart.

Papa and Gran smiled bravely. They waved as the car backed out of the driveway. Sawyer gulped back sobs as she took one last look at the little farm. Grady leaned over and brought her head to his shoulder.

"Shhh. It'll be okay, I promise, Slick. Remember, you're lucky you aren't going to China Lake in the Mojave Desert."

Grady's comment didn't comfort Sawyer. She was terrified to leave Colby, even if it meant going to Hawaii. Paradise or not, it was three thousand miles away from her friends, Gran, Papa, and everything she knew. Sawyer had never even seen the ocean. She figured everyone overrated the experience. All it meant to her was that she was a long way from home.

Bradley's new assignment was at Kaneohe Marine Base on Oahu. Sawyer couldn't pronounce it, even after Bradley told her over and over that each syllable was pronounced separately, even if it was just a vowel. It was, "Kah-nay-oh-hay." If Hawaii was as strange as its language, Sawyer wanted no part of it.

Vic wasn't there when they arrived at the border and pulled into the gas station where Grady was supposed to meet him. Bradley kept checking his watch, looking down the highway for Vic's old Volkswagen. Grady leaned against the car, head down, arms crossed. He was anxious to leave.

"Did you get through to Vic on your cell phone yet?" Bradley asked, for the third time.

"Relax dad! He'll be here soon. You can just leave me you know. I'll be fine," Grady said.

"That's not our plan, Grady, and you know it," Bradley snapped back.

The tension of the last few weeks had taken its toll on Bradley. What with graduation, the move, and the wedding, he second-guessed every decision. He was usually confident in his ability to handle any situation, but Sawyer's resigned frown, Julie's look of dismay, and Grady's eyes glued to his shoes had Bradley pacing in frustration.

In the distance, Grady finally saw Vic's black VW Bug. "Look, Dad," he sighed, "He's almost here."

Vic pulled to a stop and got out of the car stretching and smiling. "You're late!" Bradley barked.

"Sorry," Vic shrugged. "You ready for this awesome adventure, Grady?" Vic ignored the look on Bradley's face.

Grady nodded. He hoisted his duffle bag onto his shoulder and gave his dad a hurried hug. "Aloha," he said. "See you in a few weeks."

Bradley held his tongue. He didn't want to make this goodbye any more awkward. He wasn't sure Grady was ready to take off on his own, at least not with Vic. As reluctant as he was, Bradley had agreed, and he didn't go back on his word.

"Keep in touch, son. Be careful," Bradley cautioned. "I will, Dad. Don't worry so much. We'll be fine." "Have fun," Julie added, though she wasn't convinced this road trip was a good idea.

Grady leaned down to see Sawyer brooding in the backseat. "Hey, Slick, save me the best bedroom. I'm older than you. I have seniority, you know."

Sawyer couldn't help but smile a little. "Right, Grady. Take care of yourself." She stroked Gaboochie's worn-down head and gave Grady a mournful look. "I'm going to miss you," she said.

Grady's lip quivered. He put his hand through the window and patted her head just like she was patting her teddy bear. "I'll miss you too, kid," he whispered.

"Watch out for Vic," Sawyer warned. "I'm not so sure about him."

Grady's eyes darted to Vic, holding the trunk open and staring off in space. "No worries," he shrugged. "I can take care of myself."

He gave her a tap on the nose, walked over to Vic and his ancient VW Bug, and didn't look back.

CHAPTER 3

A New Home

No one was waiting at the airport terminal to greet them. There were no leis to hang around their necks, no greeting kisses. Sawyer watched their bags hurtle down the conveyor belt and wondered what her new home would be like.

They arrived on Hawaiian Air, which meant they'd landed in the remote area of the airport and had to take a Wiki Wiki tram to the baggage terminal. The heat and humidity hit Sawyer as soon as they went outside to the bus stop. The wind kept whipping strands of hair into her eyes no matter how much she pushed them away.

She decided she'd let her hair grow into a ponytail. So much for the wonderful weather everyone promised in this so-called paradise.

"You take the carry-on, Sawyer," Bradley said, as he lifted the suitcases off the carrier. Julie was loaded down with two duffel bags and her purse. They trudged to the bus stop that would take them to the car rental and hauled their stuff back and forth, until at last they reached the lot. Bradley chose a typical mid-sized car to rent until he could find a used one that would serve their needs for the next three years. Who knows where they would be sent next? Sawyer would spend middle school in Kaneohe, and then she'd have to leave after her freshman year in high school. Sometimes it seemed like forever, and then she'd decide it was no time at all.

It made her not want to bother making friends because she'd have to leave them behind so soon. Nothing could happen in those three years to make any of it worthwhile.

After they loaded the luggage, she squeezed into the small space left for her in the backseat and settled in as they headed out of the airport. There wasn't anything beautiful about the landscape. It was just like any freeway in any city. In fact, it reminded her of the view she had of Los Angeles from her window-seat on the plane, with the maze of freeways, the slow moving traffic, the little houses crammed beneath a dirty layer of smog, but here the sky was bright blue with cotton clouds that flew by in all that wind. The sky was definitely more like Kansas.

Sawyer felt another wave of homesickness. She was used to it by now. It always felt like she was going to throw up, then tears would well up in her eyes, and just as she thought she was going to lose it, the feelings would subside.

"Julie, you're in charge of navigation," Bradley said.

He handed his new wife the car rental map.

"Take the H1 to the H3 and go east," Julie said.

They started to climb as a range of steep mountains rose before them. The foliage was thick with ferns, palm trees, and other plants Sawyer had never seen before. Flowers clustered on bushes in red, yellow and delicate white. Then it started pouring out of nowhere.

"Where did that come from?" Bradley said. He seemed tempted to put on the brakes, and turned on the windshield wipers instead.

"I don't know, but it's sunny over there," Julie said.

She pointed back towards Honolulu.

The rain stopped as quickly as it started. They passed through a long tunnel cut into the mountain. When they emerged on the other side, they found themselves at the top of the mountain range looking down on the East side of the island.

The ocean curved in turquoise around coves and bays. Small islands dotted the horizon. The towns of Kaneohe and Kailua spread toward the coast. There were no high-rise buildings and no resorts, just open country and sprawling neighborhoods. The Marine Base stood on a peninsula in the distance. As Sawyer looked out her window, she was surprised to see the mountains' deep crevices flowing with water in hundred-foot drops. The waterfalls lined up one right after another in a stunning display. This Hawaiian landscape was unlike the never-ending flat plains of Kansas, or anything Sawyer had ever seen before.

They pulled up to the entrance of the base. Sawyer and Julie waited in the car while Bradley signed in and applied for a temporary parking sticker. He had told them how much tighter security was since 9/11. The driver and each passenger in the car had to be prepared to show a picture ID to get on the base. The guards were under strict orders to stop each vehicle and check each person. In spite of the inconvenience, Sawyer found it reassuring. She was glad to know that the military was taking all of these precautions to protect the men and women who served their country.

While they waited, Sawyer took in her surroundings. She saw a bronze, life-sized statue of soldiers struggling to raise a flag and tugged on her mom's sleeve to get her attention. "What is that?" she asked. Julie looked over and nodded in recognition.

"It's a copy of the statue of the seven Marines raising the American flag on Iwo Jima. It represents an important turning point in the Pacific front of World War II. The islands of the Pacific were extremely difficult to capture, so when the Marines could finally hoist the flag and declare victory, it was quite a momentous occasion." Julie sounded like a history teacher who'd just done her research. Maybe she was studying to impress Bradley.

"If you look closely," she said, "you'll see that the men represent different races too. It shows respect and cooperation." Sawyer looked at the statue where all the men were working to hoist the flag.

If she looked further past the main gate, Sawyer could just see a display of different aircraft, from old propeller planes to sleek fighter jets. She couldn't remember which ones Bradley flew, but she was sure he was going to tell her all about it. Being a Marine pilot was important to

Bradley, and he would go on and on about it if she'd let him. Whenever he talked about flying, he'd dogfight with hand gestures. Sawyer got a kick out of watching him. She could tell how much being a fighter pilot meant. There was something she remembered about this duty though, and Sawyer wasn't sure if it meant he had been demoted or promoted –more new words for her military dictionary.

When Bradley returned, he had the parking sticker and another map. Julie took over again as navigator. The Marine on duty stopped them at the main gate and they all showed their IDs. She gave a smart salute, which was kind of cool, and they were finally allowed to enter the base.

"We'll stop at the lodge, get our assignment, check out the house and unpack. Then we'll go to the Exchange to get the things we need, then stop by the Commissary for groceries," Bradley stated, in his clipped military voice.

"What's an Exchange?" Sawyer asked.

"It's an all-purpose department store, better than a discount store, but not as nice as a fancy department store."

"And the Commissary?" she continued.

"The supermarket," Bradley replied. "We also have a Mini Mart and a Package Store, which is similar to a liquor store."

Julie continued listing all the wonderful features of the base. "There's a school and a church too, but the middle school is in Kaneohe. You'll take a bus there with the other dependents."

So now Sawyer was considered a "dependent." She didn't like that word at all.

"A base is like its own self-contained town," Bradley said, "with a movie theater, a bowling alley, a golf course, and I believe this base has some fast food too."

Great, thought Sawyer. I'll never get to explore the real world!

As they drove on through the base, Sawyer saw Marines jogging on the trails and marching in formation on the fields. Mothers were taking walks with strollers and dogs in tow. Pairs of young women chatted as they crossed the busy street on the way to the Exchange.

Bradley slowed the car and pulled up to a motel.

"This is the Lodge, temporary housing for new transfers. It's also available for guests and retired military when they come to visit. We're lucky there's housing available, or we'd all be staying in one room. I know guys with their families that have had to wait over a month for permanent housing." Bradley shook his head. Sawyer's mouth hung open, feeling relieved that this was not their fate. A motel room would be way too cozy for this new family!

Bradley went in to get the housing assignment and came back with yet another map. From there, they wound their way up and into the residential part of the base. Clusters of duplexes, with yards full of children's toys and small plastic pools, stretched ahead. Then the streets grew wider, landscaped with huge trees like those in Colby. Old one-story wooden ranch-style houses sprawled out along the road. They had small fenced areas for dogs and kids too. Julie was studying the map and the Hawaiian street names, so when Bradley pulled into the driveway she was unprepared. She gasped and her eyes went wide.

"Oh, Bradley!" Julie looked ahead to find her new home on a bluff overlooking the Pacific Ocean.

"Being a Major does have its perks!" Bradley said. "The house isn't that great, but the location can't be beat." He got out of the car, took Julie in his arms and kissed her. Then he put his key into the front door lock. After quickly checking out the house, they all walked to the backyard and looked out to the endless miles of blue water. The waves tumbled to the shore. People were scattered on the beach, wandering through tide pools, sunning and surfing. Sawyer couldn't believe she'd have this to look forward to every day. Maybe this view could replace the miles of wheat fields she longed for. This ocean was magical in its own way, hypnotic and noisy.

She'd have to get used to the constant sound of waves in the background of her new life.

CHAPTER 4

Sneaking Out

If she didn't get back before light, she would be totally
busted, grounded, and who knows what else, but the idea
of exploring the beach that first night was too appealing.
Sawyer just had to do it. She crept out of her room at 2:00
AM. It felt like 7:00 AM with the 5-hour time difference.
She slipped by the newlyweds, sound asleep, and opened
the screen door to the back steps.

The houses were raised a few feet above the ground
on wooden foundations so the rain could flow through
underneath. Sawyer wondered how much it had to rain for
them to build the houses this way.

She scampered across the road and down the steps
that led to the sand. She ignored the warning signs:
"HIGH TIDE," "NO LIFEGUARD," and "CLOSED

AFTER DARK." It was worth the risk. She needed to feel independent from her new family. The sand was soft and cool on her bare feet. Lava rocks jutted out, as she got closer to the water, making it harder to walk. Something sharp jabbed into her foot and Sawyer took a deep gulp of air so she wouldn't scream. She reached down and pulled a jagged piece of shell from her heel. The sting of the salt water made her realize she was bleeding. Sawyer pressed on.

She wanted to get out on the rock formation she'd seen from the yard that afternoon. It looked like a place where a person could think, reflect, and find peace.

Sawyer needed solitude to do all three. She felt so confused. She was happy to be a family again, but she hated leaving her home in Colby, and she was scared to death of the days ahead. She worried she'd have no friends when she started school. What if there were no sports teams? What if math was impossible? What if no one talked to her, or worse, what if they were mean to her? Most of all, she missed her father's cheerful, "g'morning, Sunshine," his unwavering patience, and his bedtime stories starring Sawyer, "the glorious girl." She felt like the waves crashing over and over, all churned up with no way to stop the turmoil.

She found an impression in the cluster of rocks and sat down. The waves were spent by the time they reached her, so the water lapped at her feet. Sawyer took a deep breath, closed her eyes, willed herself not to cry again, and sighed. How did Grady go through this over and over? She didn't know how she was going to cope, knowing she'd have to do it all again in three years.

She'd just have to adjust in bite-sized pieces. This place was a good first step. The next was getting back to her room without being detected. As for tomorrow, she'd just get up, have breakfast, and go with Mom to check out the school. At least she would have some idea about where she was going when she got on the bus the first day.

Then the sky, full of stars just a few minutes before, erupted into rain. The cloudburst was as powerful as the ones in Kansas, but the drops were warmer. Sawyer was soaked, but she wasn't cold. She wondered how often this happened. Did everyone carry umbrellas or did they just go "wash and wear" all the time?

She sloshed up the stairs and snuck back to the house. No lights! Sawyer tiptoed back to her room, stripped out of her wet clothes and put on her dad's jersey. It was guaranteed to bring good dreams. Sawyer lay down on top of the covers and grabbed Gaboochie. Her last thought before she drifted off was about Grady. She wished she were his sidekick on the "Great Escape," not his sleepy-eyed buddy Vic. Sawyer hadn't been impressed by his attitude, and she didn't trust him to watch over Grady. She wondered what they were doing, then fell asleep.

CHAPTER 5

The Road Trip

Grady and Vic only made a few stops between Kansas and California. They spent one night on the edge of the Grand Canyon admiring its expanse and spectrum of colors. Grady liked the way the reflections of sunrise played on the ledges of the cliffs, but Vic preferred the hot reds and oranges of the sunset. They treated themselves to a steak and potato special at the hotel and pressed on through the desert in the cool night. The casino lights sparkled through the inky dark announcing their arrival in Vegas. They pulled into the driveway of a rundown motel whose neon sign flashed vacancy. Rooms were cheap off the strip. They took turns showering, ignored the tepid water and mold on the ancient shower curtain, and collapsed on the lumpy beds. The air conditioner rattled and gave little relief from the dry desert heat. They awoke groggy after a fitful night's sleep imagining a full day and night of gambling, but the casino bosses carded them and made it clear they'd better find a different way to entertain themselves. They figured they could get away with the quarter slots at the mini mart, but the savvy cashier confronted them, asked for IDs, and threw them out. The boys gave up their visions of striking it rich and agreed to do another all-nighter on the road.

They hit Los Angeles at rush hour and sat bumper to bumper in a sea of cars, ducking in and out of lanes, speeding up and braking as they tried to make space where there was none to be made. The freeway signs were abundant but confusing, with arrows pointing to lanes that seemed to disappear within a few feet. Grady and Vic were exhausted, but they continued on, trading off driving, desperate to get out of the traffic and the sprawling city. They wound their way south until they reached Highway 1 just below the Laguna art colony, and within an hour, Vic pulled into a parking lot in Solano Beach north of San Diego. Traffic had subsided, and they could see the beach a few feet away. They stretched their legs and climbed down to the rocky shoreline, collapsed on the sand, and watched the sunset over the glassy sea. As the sun lowered and peeked through the clouds, a burst of crimson and orange exploded in the sky. Pink streaks remained until the sun finally dove beneath the horizon in a burst of green light.

"Look at that Vic! My dad told me about the green flash over the water at sunset, but I laughed at him.

Guess I'll have to confess we saw it. He just loves being right."

"My dad, too," Vic shook his head remembering the way his dad acted like such a know-it-all. They stared at the sky trying to work up the energy to find a place to stay that night.

Grady shrugged, "Wanna just sleep in the car and get an early start tomorrow?"

Vic nodded, his eyes already drooping, and crawled into the backseat. Grady balled up his sweatshirt to use as a pillow and slumped against the window.

Feeling somewhat refreshed after sleeping in the parking lot, they headed further south to Ocean Beach, an artsy town a little north of San Diego. Vic insisted they try their luck at body surfing. Grady tumbled and spit water and sand for over an hour, then convinced Vic to take a break. They eased onto an old army blanket, aching and watching the more experienced surfers. Two skinny guys sauntered up with trunks that hung low and loose around their hips.

"Having trouble with the shore break?" The taller boy asked. He had an uneven tan and a pockmarked face. His dishwater blond hair fell to his shoulders. The other guy was shorter with a dark tan and a buzz-cut.

Vic looked up and said, "We'll figure it out." "Just trying to help. I'm Len and this is Chad. You guys spend much time catching waves?" He shaded his eyes from the harsh sun.

"I'm Grady and this is Vic. We're new to this." Grady rolled onto his side and propped himself up on one elbow.

Chad nodded. "You're diving in too late. Timing's everything."

"And you've got to do a better job of avoiding the boogie boarders," Len added. "They can get nasty if you cut in front of them."

"Thanks. Want to join us?" Vic said. He sat up to make room for them.

Grady wasn't sure about these guys. He inched to the back of the blanket as Chad and Len flopped down beside them.

"You live here?" he asked, trying to figure out if they were just being friendly or if they wanted something.

"Yeah, we have a place in O.B.," Chad said. "Where are you guys from?"

"We're on a road trip. Some friends told me this was a good place to party." Grady explained.

Chad and Len shared a smile. "You got a suggestion, Grady?"

Grady nodded. He knew about San Diego from his friends who'd been stationed at Miramar and North Island. They'd clued him in on most of the clubs in the area.

"Well," Grady said, "there's Sammy's in O.B. and a Mexican cantina in Old Town with some great margaritas. There's a bunch of clubs downtown, but the Conch Club is the best. It's supposed to be easy on IDs."

Grady savored Chad and Len's expressions as he rattled off his expansive list. He could tell they were impressed, and he was eager to keep it up. He'd never been the cool guy before.

"Why don't you guys come on back to our place?" Chad suggested. "We'll shower off this sand, pick up some beers, and take in the clubs."

Len nodded. "You can crash with us for a couple of days," he said. "Chad will even give you a few tips on body surfing."

Grady and Vic looked at each other, shrugged, and said, "Why not?"

The night started out okay. They managed to get Chad's brother to buy them a couple of six packs and drop them off on the outskirts of downtown. They sat on the sea wall drinking until a cop car cruised toward them. Chad slipped the remaining beers under his jacket and they wandered toward the bright lights of downtown. Grady claimed he knew a shortcut, but the route took them to a seedy part of the city. He led them down a narrow poorly lit street. It was late and the storefronts were dark and padlocked against intruders. In the distance, Grady could make out a flickering neon light and hoped it was the club. To be honest, they were hopelessly lost. The club he'd bragged about must be further west or maybe it didn't exist. Now they now stood on a dark corner imagining all kinds of terrible things lurking in the shadows. Without warning, an ear-piercing scream like someone being tortured echoed from deep in the alley. They flattened themselves against the side of a pawnshop, hoping to become invisible. A scrawny cat came flying out from the alley, spitting as it darted around the corner. "Catfight," they all blurted out, trying to slow their racing hearts. Chad took a swig of beer and handed the bottle to Grady. He knew if he tried to drink it, he'd throw it right up, so he set it down on the sidewalk.

Len's hand shook as he pointed to the red light down the block. They crept closer, hoping it was the club, but instead the sign read, " OPEN ALL NIGHT." A skull with a menacing grin perched on crossed swords dripping blood was painted on the window. Above it were the words, "Double Dagger."

"Jeez, Grady! Do you have any idea where we are?" Chad barked.

Grady frowned, but he said nothing. Vic nodded and said, "Open all night? Let's go in and ask about that club." They were through the door before Grady could stop them, and he reluctantly followed. A heavily tattooed and pierced man sat behind a display case filled with strange knives, and swords.. His greasy black hair hung limp and covered one eye. His skin had the pasty look of someone who rarely saw the sun. Two rings pierced one nostril, joined by a fine chain. "What's up?" he rasped.

"We're looking for the Conch Club," Grady replied with a weak, scratchy voice as he stepped forward.

"Ah, the cops shut it down about a year ago. It had a reputation for not checking IDs," the man snickered.

As Grady turned to go, the man added, "Wanna buy an authentic Samurai sword?" He pointed to a tarnished weapon with a carved hilt that rested on a red silk scarf in the case. As Grady shook his head, his eyes fell on the man's bare shoulder. It was tattooed with the same sword. Blood dripped off the end of the blade and pooled on the chest of a fallen tiger.

"Then, how about a tattoo, kid? It's a better way to spend your allowance than at some club and a permanent souvenir to boot."

Grady shook his head, but the others latched on to the idea. Some excitement had to come out of this dismal adventure.

"Yeah Grady, you're going to Hawaii, you need a tattoo to fit in with the locals," Vic laughed.

Chad pulled up his shirt to show off his upper arm and shoulder. "I got this because I'm so hilarious."

Skulls dangled from the points of the grinning jester's triangular cap. Chad's tattoo wasn't much of an endorsement.

"You've got an ID that says your eighteen, right?"

The man's eyebrows rose and he gave Grady a sly grin. Pick one of those designs off the wall and I'll do it for half price. If you want an original, it'll take longer, and I charge a design fee up front." His pitch wasn't convincing, but everyone besides Grady chimed in with their support.

Grady flinched. His head ached from the beer and his empty stomach churned, but he hoped the tattoo would redeem his club fiasco. Maybe a tattoo was just what he needed.

He turned his eyes to the wall covered in sketches, pen and ink drawings, and photos of skulls, coiled snakes, majestic eagles, Navy anchors, and even familiar cartoon characters. Only one design had the right combination of restraint and artistic flare. Strange unfamiliar characters interlocked with red flames that would curve up Grady's calf. The bottom of the fire arced into a pointed tail. It wasn't too small, like the token butterflies or dolphins the tourist girls would get. Grady wasn't sure what drew him to it, but he liked it better than the other options.

"I'll take that one with the flames," Grady blurted out.

"Cool." Vic smiled at the others.

The boys followed the man into a back room and Grady lay down on the scratchy vinyl padded table, cracked from overuse, and pulled up his pant leg to expose his calf. "What's the story behind the tattoo I picked?" he asked. He was dreading the pain to come, desperate to put it off just a little while longer.

"A burly Asian guy came in with a picture of it. He was a martial artist, and he had the scars to prove it. I did the work and he said he would be back for more, but he

never showed up. Typical in this business," he said. His voice tapered off as he swiped a wet paper towel across Grady's leg, then shaved the spot to work his magic.

The sound of the tattoo machine reminded Grady of the dentist's chair, the drill pressing on a cavity in his back molar. The pain was intense as the needles vibrated and penetrated his skin. His face was down so he couldn't see his friends, but their moans did nothing to comfort him.

"Look at all those beads of blood," Vic whispered to Chad.

"Gnarly," Chad whispered back.

The artist used the same scratchy towel to dab the blood, now mixed with the red of the flames. He did the writing with an even wider group of needles to make the thick black lines. Grady clenched his teeth, determined not to cry out.

It was almost dawn when the four of them staggered up the steep stairs to Chad and Len's old stucco apartment in a weedy lot behind the liquor store. The living room was furnished with garage sale specials and empty beer bottles littered the floor. The couch where he was supposed to sleep was stained and threadbare, but he was too tired to care.

When he looked at his shaved leg, he saw the film of Vaseline and dots of blood still bubbling over his new tattoo. Grady stared at the image. Lots of Marines had them, so the idea wasn't totally foreign to Grady. Chad had that jester on his forearm, and he claimed he was getting a dragon after he got paid. Vic egged him on, making him feel like he had to do it. Grady just didn't want his friends to think he was a loser so he had caved. Now it was done and there was no way to undo it.

He dozed off on the cramped couch, wondering how his family was adjusting to Hawaii. Those thoughts soon faded from his mind as he felt himself drifting down into a dark hole. He was spinning, falling fast, and just catching glimpses of the swirling shapes. They twisted and turned in a spiral of flames. There was a gaping mouth that snarled as its forked tongue darted out, and its twin prongs reaching to pluck out his eyes. The heat of its breath felt like an open furnace. He fell back into a cloud of fog and awoke with a start, sweating, his mind cluttered with horrible images. He looked around him. The only light in the room came from a scummy aquarium, crawling with tarantulas. "What's happening to me?" he mumbled.

CHAPTER 6

Checking Out

It was too early, 6:00 AM, and Sawyer was already awake. In Kansas it would be 11:00 AM, which was late for her, even on a lazy morning. She walked out the back door and watched the sun rise over the ocean. Their house faced east, not west like in Kansas, so she'd have to get used to seeing the sunrise instead of the sunset up close. Eventually, she'd adjust to the time change and sleep in like a normal kid.

Julie puttered around in the kitchen, making lists of things she needed to cook a decent meal. They were waiting for their shipment from home to arrive, full of necessities and treasures. Maybe Gran's red polka-dot quilt or Sawyer's collection of baseball caps would make the place feel more like home. Until then, it was back to basics. Sawyer finished her cereal, tipped her head back for the last of the milk, and then tossed the paper bowl and plastic spoon into the trashcan. She pumped her fist as they landed in the wastebasket. "Two points!" she cheered. "When are we going to school, Mom?" Sawyer was anxious to get it over with.

"We'll leave as soon as I finish this last list," Julie said.

In short order, the two of them ran through another downpour, jumped into the rental car, and backtracked to the main gate. Once they crossed the lagoon, they followed the map to Kaneohe Middle School. Sawyer was disappointed to see a dingy old building with peeling paint and potholes in the schoolyard pavement. Its only redeeming feature was a mural painted on the front of the building. The students must've worked together to create a panorama of the island, both above and below the water. The ocean floor was decorated with gnarled coral, pink shells, and silky green seaweed. The depths of the water were a deep blue that graduated to turquoise in the middle and pale aqua at the surface. Sleek black and yellow striped fish swam in schools as others in brilliant blue and orange were tucked among the seaweed. Jellyfish floated just below the surface and a shark knifed through the center of the mural, its jaws wide open. Kayaks raced on the waves above and wind surfers skimmed by. Small island peaks dotted the horizon. The sky was packed with clouds, storms and sunshine, gulls, egrets, and even cranes swooping down to the ocean's surface.

Julie and Sawyer made their way to the office and introduced themselves to the girl at the desk. She was

Sawyer's age, but she seemed to be in charge. She was a dark-eyed with warm brown skin and black hair that hung straight to her waist.

"We're the Sommers," Julie said. "This is my daughter Sawyer, who'll be attending in the fall. We have an appointment with the principal, and we'd also like a tour of the campus if that's possible."

"Aloha!" The girl at the desk gave a striking smile. "E komo mai, welcome to our school! My name is Kaleʻa. I'm the student intern this summer, and I'd be happy to show you around. When we get back, our principal will talk to you and get your classes set up."

Kaleʻa escorted them out the door and down the hall to the lockers. They were stacked three high. "Seventh graders have to take the high ones," she explained. "The older students have seniority. Dumb, isn't it?" Sawyer worried she wouldn't be able to reach the lock or read her combination. How was she going to get to the back of that locker without some tall person's help? She tried not to stress out about it, but really, what was she supposed to do?

After a quick look at the classrooms, the cafeteria, and the art center, Sawyer found the gym. She asked about a few things along the way, but now she was ready with plenty of questions.

"What sports teams do you have? Is there track for girls? When does it start? Do we have P.E. every day?"

"Are you a jock?" Kaleʻa asked.

"I guess so. I mean, I really like sports. I ran track at home and played some soccer," Sawyer said. She tried to sound humble but there was a twinge of pride in her voice.

"Cool! I play soccer too, and I run the half-mile during track season. I bet we'll end up working out together. The sports program is after school. Some of the teams are pretty weak, like baseball," Kaleʻa rolled her eyes, "but the track program is great. Coach Torres is tough on us, but it pays off. We win all the time, especially against Kailua, the town next to us. They're the Sharks, our biggest rival." Kaleʻa threw her shoulders back with an air of authority.

Rain started to float down from dark clouds as they returned to the office. "Ah, it's a blessing," Kaleʻa murmured.

"A blessing?" Julie and Sawyer asked in unison. "In Hawaii, we learn to appreciate the rains. They keep our island green and beautiful. It's refreshing when it's hot out," Kaleʻa shrugged.

They dashed into the office, wet from the blessing.

It took almost an hour to go through Sawyer's schedule. The principal answered all her questions about academics with as much patience as she could muster.

Finally, she led them out and past the counter where Kaleʻa was sorting through class schedules. She handed Sawyer a piece of paper with her phone number written on it.

Kaleʻa asked, "Why don't you come to a party I'm having for the 4ᵗʰ of July next week? You can meet some of my friends, and all you have to do is bring a pūpū!" Sawyer didn't have the courage to ask what a "pūpū" was.

"Thank you so much for showing me around!" Sawyer said. "I'd love to come to your party and meet all your friends."

"We say Mahalo," Kaleʻa replied. When Sawyer cocked her head in confusion, Kaleʻa laughed and said, "It's Hawaiian for thank you."

"Well then, mahalo, Kaleʻa," Sawyer grinned. "I'll call you as soon as we get our phone." They waved goodbye.

Sawyer and her mom climbed back in the car. They were quiet as they put on their seatbelts and absorbed everything they'd seen that day. Julie turned to her daughter. They raised their eyebrows at each other.

Sawyer's lips turned up into a slight smile as they asked in unison, "What's a pūpū?" They broke into uncontrollable laughter. Holding their stomachs, their eyes watering, the tension of the last few days faded a little. Sawyer and her mom finished their good laugh with a shrug. They had a new priority at the top of the list. It was time to figure out what a "pūpū" was.

CHAPTER 7

Grady's Decision

Grady staggered as he pushed himself up from the couch. He looked out the window and saw only a dense blanket of fog. All the changes throughout the last few years weighed him down. He missed his dad. He kept imagining the smell of cornbread pancakes and bacon that his father would cook on Sunday mornings. He wondered where his mother was right now. Maybe she was at her yoga class or visiting one of her friends. She hated the military life with all those rules and expectations. She worried about his father the whole time they were married, especially when he was flying combat missions. She pictured him getting shot down, making a pilot error, or the plane malfunctioning. She'd seen the black car pull up in front of a neighbor's house, watched the chaplain walk to the front door, heard him deliver the dreaded news, and shivered as a military wife just like her broke down in the doorway. They all lived in fear of the words, "missing in action," or "killed in the line of duty," but his mom always anticipated she would be next. The stress and loneliness eroded their marriage. Grady could understand why she left, but he just couldn't figure out why she didn't want to take him with her. He talked to his mom every month and visited her during the summer sometimes, but they weren't close.

She seemed to go on with her life just fine without him. He tried not to mind too much, but he missed having a mother. He wasn't sure how Julie was going to fit into his life, but she couldn't be his mom. As for Sawyer, she was cooler than he thought she'd be. At first he figured she'd just be a pain he'd have to endure, but she was tough. He tried to get the best of her with his wrestling moves, but she hung in there and even Julie understood that he was just giving her a little test of character like big brothers do.

Grady looked down at his leg. He wasn't sure what to expect. The tattoo was inflamed and oozed blood from the deep black lines that formed the characters. He tried to rub in some more Vaseline, but it was sore and hot to the touch. He hoped it wasn't infected. The tattoo artist was unclear about how to take care of it, or how long it would take to heal. He felt filthy after sleeping on the dirty couch and sweating from the nightmare. There was still sand between his toes and the remnants of salt crusted on his heals from yesterday's body boarding.

He needed a shower, but the guy told him not to get the tattoo wet for a while. Grady hobbled into the kitchen, wet a paper towel in the sink and rubbed it over his tired face. He was ready to cut his road trip short and catch the next available plane to Hawaii. He hated to admit it, but he was homesick and a little scared.

Vic wandered in from the bedroom. He'd slept on the floor with a beach towel for a blanket. Dark bags hung under grumpy eyes.

"Hey dude, I'm done with this road trip," Grady confessed.

"You're crazy! Can't handle all this freedom, huh?" Vic snapped.

"Guess not. I'm the one who ended up with a tattoo."

Vic checked out Grady's leg and his voice lowered to a whisper. "Looks nasty," he said.

Grady's jaw tensed. He glared at Vic. By the time the others straggled in, Grady had already called the airline and made his reservation. Vic decided to stay in Ocean Beach with Chad and Len. Grady worried about his friend, but he was more worried about himself. It was going to be tough to explain the tattoo, but he'd just have to face it. He needed to get back to his family.

CHAPTER 8

Kaleʻa's Party

Julie pulled into an officer's parking spot and walked up to the entrance of the Commissary. Though she felt a little foolish, Julie knew finding out the definition of a "pūpū" was important to Sawyer. She showed her ID to the woman in charge, and since she appeared to be Hawaiian, took a chance and asked, "Could you please tell me where I can find a pūpū?"

"What kind of pūpūs are you looking for?" The woman sounded a bit put out by the question.

"There's more than one kind?" Julie was stumped. "I'm new to Hawaii. I'm supposed to bring a pūpū for a teenager's party, but I have no idea what it is," she admitted.

"A pūpū is an appetizer, a snack, maybe just a bag of chips and dip. If you want something fancy, you can get poke, but kids are probably gonna be happier with something simple."

She knew she'd never impress Kaleʻa and her friends with a bag of chips. She wanted to ask what poke was, but then she'd look even dumber than she already felt. Julie's look of bewilderment softened the woman. "Poke is raw fish in a soy-based sauce," she said.

Julie shook her head. She wasn't ready to tackle slimy raw fish. "Thank you," she sighed, feeling defeated, and pushed her cart to the first aisle. She decided to buy a variety of Sawyer's favorite party snacks and hope for the best.

She came home from the Commissary with new information and a bag of groceries containing numerous pūpū options. Sawyer wanted to bring something fun, a little different, but not too fancy. They settled on spicy buffalo wings. Gran made a plate of them for her last birthday in Colby and they were a big hit. She could still picture her friends sucking the sauce from their fingers.

Sawyer changed her clothes three times before she ended up in her favorite jean shorts, a red tank top with a yellow peace sign, and her cleanest tennis shoes. It was too hot for anything else.

"You look ready to party," Bradley said, looking up from a mound of papers on the kitchen table. He'd been so busy, there was barely any time to talk. She wondered if it would always be like this. She hoped he could relax a little when he settled in and officially took charge of his new squadron. Maybe he'd even take her on a special tour of the base. She was curious about the military with all its rules and customs. Most of the Marines saluted each other, but not all of them. Did it have to do with rank, age, or maybe uniforms? She wanted to ask him about the strange half-buried buildings in the hillsides.

She knew they must have some particular use. Bradley would know the answer. There were so many questions, but he seemed preoccupied, and she felt too shy to interrupt. He'd been such a good listener in Kansas, but now more important duties took up his time, and it felt like he'd lost interest in her.

"Be careful tonight," Bradley said. "Don't let the Hawaiian kids give you a hard time. They do that sometimes, especially if you're military. Hawaiians are suspicious of foreigners, and it's true that we don't always show the proper respect."

Sawyer hadn't thought about that. She was in the minority here, and the other kids might be prejudiced against her. She'd never had to deal with something like that before. Her stomach lurched.

Julie gave Bradley a stern look. He had a way of saying the right thing, but at the wrong time, and she was afraid his comment would make Sawyer even more reluctant to go. She placed her hand on her daughter's shoulder.

"You'll be fine with Kaleʻa there to introduce you," Julie said. "She seems like a lovely girl. Just be yourself and you'll have a great time."

With their map in hand again, Julie and Sawyer drove off in search of a street called Mokanami. They almost missed the street sign, disguised beneath a swaying palm. Julie made a hard right and crept through the palms and vines down the gravel road that ended at the bay. The house was perched on stilts, balanced precariously over the shore. Sawyer was expecting ukeleles, but rock music poured from the doorway. She gripped her pūpū tray of buffalo wings and kissed her mom on the cheek.

"I'll call you when I'm ready to come home," she said, a little breathless.

"Don't be too late," Julie called back as she slowly made a U-turn and drove back up the gravel path.

She paused at the top of the driveway and put her head down on the steering wheel. Her nerves were frayed. She hoped the kids would accept Sawyer for the great kid she was. Rain started pelting the windshield and she sat back up. She worried she'd been idealizing her marriage. It was hard to be a military wife, harder than she'd expected. Bradley was concerned about his new position and it reflected in his attitude. He seemed to be distancing himself from both of them. Julie was determined to be understanding, but she needed to remind him that she and Sawyer were new to this. They deserved more of his time and attention. She leaned back in her seat, brushed a stray tear from her face, and tried to put her doubts on hold. Finally, she turned on the wipers, pulled out onto the road, and headed back to the base.

Sawyer stepped through the open door and over a pile of sandals. She didn't see Kaleʻa. The room was empty but she could hear voices coming from the deck. Her eyes darted from side to side as she tried to take in everything at once. A painting hung on the living room wall, a sea in bold brush strokes of royal blue, a beach alive in lemon yellow and slashes of gold. A barefoot woman in a flowered sarong walked away from the viewer, leaving footprints in the sand. Her hair fell to her waist, and her head was turned like someone just called her name. Under the painting was a dragon sculpture carved of wood the size of a tree trunk. A thick piece of glass balanced on its tail to make a tabletop where a sweet scented candle burned in an abalone shell. Sawyer was tempted to linger, but she forced herself to continue through the house to the deck that overlooked the bay.

"Hey Sawyer!" Kale'a called out from a group in the corner. She made her way over, looked her up and down, and then settled her eyes on her shoes. "I'm glad you could come," she said, then pushed Sawyer back into the house as gently as she could.

Sawyer had a bad feeling that Kale'a was hiding her from the rest of the party. Kale'a took the pūpū tray, set it on the counter near the kitchen, and nudged Sawyer all the way back to the front door.

"In Hawaii, we take our shoes off when we enter a home. Everyone takes it pretty seriously. That's one reason we always wear slippers. It's easy to slip them on and off." Kale'a giggled at her own play-on-words.

"Oh, what a relief," Sawyer sighed. "I thought you changed your mind about me." She took off her shoes and socks and tossed them into the pile on the floor.

None of the other sandals were fuzzy like her red Santa slippers, but she got the picture. Sawyer smiled. "Guess I need to buy some slippers soon," she mumbled.

They laughed and headed back to the kitchen. Kaleʻa introduced Sawyer to her parents, who were tearing pork from the bone, the traditional main course for a luau.

Her mother scooted around from the kitchen island with her greasy hands up in the air and attempted to give Sawyer a proper hug without smearing pork juice on her. "Aloha, Sawyer!" she gave her a peck on each cheek. "You can call me Jasmine, and this is Charlie. We're real informal on the island, and we're so happy you could join us," she said. Her husband was a wiry man not much taller than Kaleʻa. He was shirtless and had a tattoo that covered his entire back. Sawyer didn't want to stare, but she was fascinated by the intricate octopus that stretched from his shoulder blades to his waist.

"Thank you," Sawyer said. "Your home is beautiful. It's almost like being in a jungle."

"We like the privacy, and of course, the view of the bay is awesome." Jasmine pointed behind her. "I understand your family is stationed at the Marine Base."

"We just got here. I'm not sure how long we'll stay," Sawyer dropped her eyes.

"Moving's difficult," Jasmine nodded. "My mom's from the North Shore. Her family came from the Philippines to work the sugar plantations. My dad's Hawaiian. When he joined the Navy, he was stationed at Pearl Harbor. We were lucky they extended him. No one else could do his job. He's retired now, but he still lives in Honolulu. I didn't leave the island until I went to college on the Mainland," Jasmine rambled.

"What made you come back?" Sawyer asked.

"I met Charlie, when I came home for Christmas vacation my senior year. When I finished school, I applied for a professorship at the University of Hawaii." Jasmine smiled at Charlie, "That way I could come home to my kealoha."

"That's Hawaiian for beloved," Kale'a rolled her eyes, "Really mom."

"Wow, what do you teach?" Sawyer was impressed by Jasmine's decisions.

"Japanese cultural studies," Jasmine replied. Her eyes sparkled with pride.

"Are you in the military too?" Sawyer asked Charlie. She couldn't imagine him in uniform.

"No," he laughed. "I have a fleet of fishing boats. I catch Ono, Ahi, and Mahi Mahi for the local restaurants."

"If your family likes fish, we'll send some home with you after the party," Jasmine offered.

"That would be great. I mean, mahalo," Sawyer stuttered.

Jasmine smiled. "Keep at it," she chuckled. "You're learning."

Kale'a picked up Sawyer's tray of buffalo wings. "Mmm, looks yummy!" she said. She led Sawyer away before she could say anything more or get a better look at Charlie's tattoo. They met a boy in the hallway, taller than Kale'a, but with the same hair and the same eyes.

It'd be easier to see the family connection if he was smiling, but he scowled at Sawyer.

"Sawyer, this is my brother, Kanoa."

Kanoa kept glaring at them, mumbled some kind of greeting, and walked out the front door in a huff. Kaleʻa shook her head with a look of disgust on her face.

"I'm sorry, Sawyer. He doesn't think much of newcomers, or little sisters either. Come on out to the lānai and meet some of my friends. You'll like them."

Hmm, so a deck is called a lānai Sawyer thought and tucked it into her memory bank. She kept thinking about Bradley's warnings and Grady's past experiences. Her hands were damp and her smile was a bit forced as she followed behind Kaleʻa.

The lānai was crowded. Only a few people glanced up as Sawyer and Kaleʻa joined the party and put the tray on the buffet table. Small groups were scattered about, drinks in-hand or balancing plates of pūpūs, some deep in conversation, and others staring over the bay. Sawyer was reminded of the huge differences among kids her age. Some girls were tall and curvy, but others were short and skinny like she was. Some boys were scrawny and some were hefty. Most had dark hair, but that's where the similarities ended. Most of their ancestors were Hawaiian, Japanese, Chinese, Filipino, and even Samoan. With more than 200 years of intermarriage, the combinations were endless. Sawyer worried she wouldn't be able to tell who was from where, but how much did it all matter, really? She wished she'd asked Bradley more questions so she could be better prepared.

They joined a group of three pretty girls wearing tight tank tops and low-slung skirts in beautiful Hawaiian patterns. Standing next to them made Sawyer feel like a little kid. The girls looked down at her and said, "Hi," in unison.

Kale'a looked uncomfortable as she said, "'Olina, Amy, Lani, this is Sawyer. She will be in our class in the fall."

"Where are you from?" 'Olina asked. Black bangs framed her almond eyes. She had high cheekbones and an indifferent smirk. She wore a bright yellow top and a red hibiscus in her hair.

"Kansas," Sawyer sputtered. What happened to my voice? She thought. The words just didn't want to come out of her mouth.

"That's, like, on the mainland, right?" Amy asked.

She chewed on a piece of gum, blew bubbles, and snapped them one after another. The sound was so annoying that Sawyer had to turn her head and focus on the ocean. Gran always said that when you smacked on your gum, you looked like a cow chewing its cud. She suppressed a snicker at the image.

"Sawyer's mom just married a Major and they're stationed at the Marine Base," Kale'a explained. She forced a smile.

"So you're military." Lani glanced at 'Olina with a knowing look on her face. Sawyer looked over to Kale'a, thinking, What's going on? Kale'a shook her head. Sawyer knew what that meant: "I'll tell you later." 'Olina was the obvious leader of the clique, and the others followed her lead. "Bet your new dad's pretty strict, being a Marine and all," she said.

Sawyer shrugged, "He's been okay so far."

"Just wait." Lani tossed back her long black hair and all three nodded, like they knew Bradley better than she did. "The military's all the same. Rules and regulations." Sawyer was about to disagree, but 'Olina chimed in before she could.

"Well, good luck with your new family." 'Olina turned her back on Sawyer, put her hand up to shield her mouth and whispered a comment to her friends alone.

They all giggled as they walked away.

They left Sawyer edgy. None of them looked like they were her age, and they acted like they were superior to everyone else. Sawyer had just bought her first training bra, but she still felt more mature than they were. She was angry with herself for getting intimidated and not standing up for Bradley. His military attitude might be hard to take sometimes, but she knew he was trying. Sawyer dreaded the another introduction, but she was determined not to let the next person get the best of her.

"Don't mind them," Kale'a whispered in her ear. "They think they're so hot, but all they do is talk about boys, clothes, and parties."

"We had a few like that in Colby." Sawyer was thankful Kale'a could see them for who they were.

"Yeah, my mom and dad said I had to invite the whole class, but we ignore each other at school," Kale'a added.

They moved on to a couple of dark-haired guys draped over the railing, tossing ice cubes into the bay. They wore baggy shorts and sleeveless t-shirts, and Sawyer couldn't help but notice their tanned, muscular legs and shoulders.

"What in the world are you doing?" Kaleʻa asked. "Seeing if we can get that crab to move," one of the boys answered.

Kaleʻa and Sawyer joined them. They leaned over the rail to see a fist-sized crab sitting on a rock ten feet below. The boys dug their fingers into their drinks to find the largest ice cubes and took turns pelting him.

"You're a lousy shot, Mike," Tony said, as Mike's cube ricocheted off the rock and into the water.

"Like you can do better?" Mike challenged.

The dare was enough to improve his aim. Tony's next cube was a direct hit and bounced off the crab's back.

"Bull's eye!" they shouted. The crab decided it'd had enough. It crawled off the rock and into the surf. The boys high-fived and turned their attention to Sawyer and Kaleʻa.

"You guys are lōlō." Kaleʻa spun her finger around her ear. Sawyer knew what that meant, crazy. "This is Sawyer. These are my surfing buddies, Mike and Tony."

Tony looked her over suspiciously. She was kind of small and skinny, she didn't have much of a tan, and she looked like she wished she were somewhere else. "Cool shirt," he said, and gave her the peace sign.

Mike didn't have much use for girls, but he trusted Kaleʻa's judgment. "You surf?" he asked.

"Not yet, but I'd like to learn," Sawyer said. "Bring her to Cockroach on Thursday," Mike said.

Tony nodded, but he quirked an eyebrow. He couldn't believe his friend was inviting this newcomer to their sacred spot.

"We'll give her a lesson. Make sure she wears a rash guard." Mike nudged Sawyer's bony ribcage with his elbow. "How's your balance?" he asked.

Sawyer didn't lose her footing or her cool. "Sounds like a blast," she said, and gave them her most casual shrug.

Tony shook his head at the prospect of teaching this newcomer to surf. "I hope you're a good swimmer," he said. The boys turned away, tossed the remains of their drinks over the rail, and headed to the pūpū table with their empty plates and cups.

Sawyer watched them go. Those snooty girls weren't worth worrying about, but Mike and Tony were okay.

She took a deep breath and stood a little taller. She was going to be outgoing, friendly, and confident. Kaleʻa grabbed her arm and said, "Come on and meet Jenna. You'll like her."

A girl stood alone by the open door. Her eyes scanned the lānai as she leaned against the doorjamb. She was long-legged with curly red hair and a face full of freckles. When she saw Kaleʻa walking towards her, she broke into a grin and waved. Sawyer thought she'd found a kindred spirit. This girl looked as uncomfortable as Sawyer felt.

"Hey Jenna!" Kaleʻa said. "I'm so glad you could make it. This is my new friend, Sawyer." Kaleʻa turned to Sawyer. "We play on the same soccer team," she explained. "She loves soccer too."

"Great to meet you, Sawyer!" Jenna said. "Do you play offense? You look kinda small for defense."

"I play left wing most of the time, but I like center forward too." Sawyer tried not to take the comment about her size too personally. "How about you?"

"I usually get stuck with fullback. I have a big kick, but my passing's not so great." She looked down, embarrassed. She remembered her last game, where the opposing team stole the ball from her over and over again as she tried to move it down field.

"Come on Jenna, your passing has really improved," Kaleʻa encouraged her with a quick hug.

Jenna hugged her back. "You're sweet. I love to play, but we both know I'm not very good. Kaleʻa and I are on a team together this summer. I need to improve a lot to make our school team this year," Jenna frowned as she spoke.

"Kaleʻa told me the team is wins a lot. I hope I can make it too." Sawyer's heart beat a little faster, worried that she wasn't tall enough or skilled enough to make the team either.

"Maybe we can get together and practice," Jenna suggested. Sawyer could tell she wanted to be included, and it felt good to know that someone wanted to be her friend.

"Sure!" Sawyer said.

The three of them wandered over to the pūpū table and Sawyer poured a well-deserved soda. She overheard Mike telling Tony about the "awesome buffalo wings" and smiled, then glanced down to the tray to see only a few remaining.

As she surveyed the party, she couldn't help but stare at a pretty girl in a wheelchair surrounded by a group of boys and girls. "Who is that?" she asked.

"That's Amanda. She's the brainiac of the group and super funny too."

They walked over and heard the end of her explanation of the migration of whales. The sun was setting and glowed brightly behind Amanda's chair. Kale'a shaded her eyes and introduced Sawyer to the group. Their nods were friendly enough, but Amanda's genuine smile and outreached hand really got her attention. She shook it delicately as she could tell it was an effort for Amanda to lift it.

"Aloha Sawyer," Amanda's face lit up when she spoke. "How do you like Hawaii so far?"

"It's pretty cool." Sawyer didn't want to go into detail about all the challenges of a new family and a new home.

"You must get so homesick," Amanda nodded in sympathy. "We'll all try to show you the ropes." She looked at those around her, "Won't we guys?"

Everyone nodded and Sawyer smiled in gratitude.

Kale'a spotted two other boys and said, "Come on, I want you to meet two of my oldest friends." She beckoned Sawyer to follow her to the far side of the lānai.

Sawyer walked with a little more confidence after her experiences with Jenna and Amanda.

The boys smiled at Kale'a as they approached and looked at Sawyer with curiosity. One of them was huge in every way, from his height to his belly to his plump cheeks. The other boy was his opposite, just a shade taller than Sawyer, with bony legs and a pinched, bird-like face. Only his feet were big. They reminded Sawyer of flippers.

"What's up?" the pudgy boy asked.

"I want you to meet Sawyer. She's new to the island." Kaleʻa smiled at both boys. "Sawyer, this is Kōnane and Mauananui. We've known each other forever. Our moms hang out a lot."

The boys nodded without giving away who was who. Sawyer was about to say, "Nice to meet you," but Kōnane interrupted her before she got a chance.

"Your name's weird," he said. He ignored Kaleʻa's dirty look.

"My mom loved Tom Sawyer," Sawyer said. "She wanted me to be adventurous, so she named me after him. I used to hate it, but now I'm used to it."

"Who's Tom Sawyer?" Kōnane asked.

"My name means Big Mountain," Mauananui blurted out.

Sawyer turned pink with embarrassment. She decided to keep Tom Sawyer's history to herself. Maybe it was time to seek out a friendlier group.

"Are you sure it doesn't mean big mound?" Kaleʻa laughed. She gave Nui a punch in the arm and patted his ample belly. That seemed to loosen the tension. Sawyer sighed. She was grateful for Kaleʻa's good humor.

Kaleʻa quickly changed the subject. "Sawyer's a jock. She plays soccer and runs track." Both boys perked up.

"Do you run sprints or long distance?" Nui asked. "Long distance, the mile and two mile. How about you?" Sawyer was happy they had something in common.

"Coach makes me run the half mile, but shot-put is my favorite event," Nui said.

"I can see why," Sawyer nodded, "You look really strong."

Nui beamed at the compliment.

Kōnane was determined to get his fair share of attention.

"I specialize in high jump. I can do the Fosburry flop."

Nui snorted. "That's only 'cause you're so short." "Oh yeah?" Konana said. "You're so big you're always bringing up the rear, slowpoke!" Kale'a stepped in.

"Ko won the Rookie of the Year award last spring. It was awesome. Believe it or not, he can jump his own height." Kale'a gave him a pat on the back.

"Congratulations, Kōnane!" Sawyer said. "Our team never had a high jumper do that."

"You can call me Ko. Most of my friends do." He gave her a bashful look.

"Cool." Sawyer sighed. An explosion interrupted their conversation, and a flash lit up the sky to begin the fireworks display. Sawyer was glad to have a break. She watched as the multi-colored streams of light reflected on the bay. She felt shaky this evening, sometimes downright awful, but she was encouraged, too. As it turned out, Hawaii kids were a lot like Kansas kids.

CHAPTER 9

Grady Lands

Sawyer wanted to bring a lei to the airport, but she thought Grady might think it was dumb. Instead, she just stood there with a grin waiting for him to get off the Wiki Wiki tram. Bradley and Mom sent her into the baggage area while they circled the car through the airport traffic maze. Sawyer was proud she'd be the first family member Grady would see. She spotted him as he made his way off the tram. Sawyer was shocked by his appearance. He winced with each step. His eyelids were crusty and pink and it looked like he'd lost a lot of weight, but she ran over, waving frantically, shouting, "Grady, Grady, over here!"

"Ah, Slick, you look great. Wow, you're so tan! How are Dad and Julie getting along?" Grady gave her a long hug. He stank of deodorant, body odor, salt water, and stale beer.

"We're all good, but Grady, what happened to you? Are you sick? Is that why you came home early?"

Beads of sweat slid down Grady's face. He was too pale. He wasn't standing tall like the Grady she remembered. His shoulders slumped and he had a bit of a limp when he walked.

"I'm okay," he said. "Just tired. I haven't slept much, but I'm glad to be here." He ruffled her hair and picked up his duffle bag. They headed to the curb.

It was way too quiet in the car. Sawyer suspected something was really wrong. She talked about the weather, their view of the ocean, and her new friend Kale'a, but it all seemed to fall on deaf ears. Grady kept closing his eyes and jerking them open with a strange look on his face. They pulled into the driveway and Grady looked out to the ocean beyond. "Cool," he said, but he showed no enthusiasm. He noticed his bike parked in the carport and gave the seat an absent pat as he went by "Where's my room?"

Sawyer led Grady down the hall to his bedroom. She remembered his comment about seniority and picked the room with the best view for him. She'd made the bed with the sheets Bradley said were his, but Grady didn't seem to notice.

"I'll be out in a while. I need to try to get a nap. It was a long flight and I'm pretty tired." Grady slumped down on the bed.

"Okay. I'll turn on the fan. You'll need the air blowing. It gets real hot and stuffy in here." Sawyer pulled the chain and the fan began to whirl overhead.

"Thanks Slick." Grady lowered himself onto the bed and closed his eyes.

Sawyer shut the door and stared at it. How did Grady change so much in such a short period of time? She was convinced something happened on his road trip and was determined to get to the truth as soon as Grady settled in.

CHAPTER 10

The Big Reveal

Grady was exhausted. He tried all the tricks he knew to relax and let his mind go blank, but nothing was working. Still awake, he stared at the blackness behind closed eyes, listened to the repetitive sound of the waves and the whir of the fan. He took deep breaths and counted them, but it was no use. He kept picturing the long flickering tongue, the fiery breath, and the teeth like jagged pieces of glass. He gave up on sleep and limped to the window. The day blustered with clouds that blocked the sun, but the room was hot and humid. It seemed like too much effort to get up, go out, and face his family. He knew the tattoo had a lot to do with it. It was too hot to keep it covered up with cellophane. There was no way he was pulling jeans over it again. The stiff denim chafed his raw skin, now swollen and red. He shook his head, put on a pair of shorts, and peeled away the cellophane to let the wound breathe. Grady opened the door and headed to the living room, resigned to the inevitable battle with his father. Better to get it over with and move on.

Grady strolled into the kitchen. His dad and Julie were busy chopping bell peppers and mushrooms for dinner. Sawyer turned and grinned when she saw him.

"Hey Grady, did you get some sleep?"

"Naw, but I did rest for a while. It sure is hot here!"

Bradley watched his son as he opened the fridge to search for a snack. His eyes fell to Grady's leg and he stiffened in horror. Bradley squinted hard and exploded before Julie could reply. "That's a tattoo on your leg! What the hell were you thinking?"

"I got it in San Diego," Grady shrugged. "Lots of people have them."

"I can't tell what it is," Sawyer added. She tried to get a better look at the artwork.

"It's just a design I liked," Grady mumbled. "What does it say?" Julie asked.

"I don't know," Grady admitted.

"You put this on your body forever, and you don't even know what it says?" Bradley shook his head. He was trying to contain himself, but it wasn't doing much good. Grady wanted to say something smart and walk out the door, but all he could manage was to slouch his shoulders and look down. "Lots of Marines have them, Dad. What's the big deal?"

"What's the big deal?" He slammed the knife down on the cutting board. His fists were clenched and his knuckles were white. Grady could tell he was fighting to keep his face from turning red.

"You're too young and you have no idea what you're doing. Most Marines choose symbols that are important

to them. You don't even know what your tattoo says. You're going to spend a long time trying to cover that thing up or remove it, if you can, and let me tell you something else – you're going to regret it." He was about to go on until he saw Julie and Sawyer's faces, warning him to back off. Grady dropped his eyes, and then snapped them back into his father's.

"Oh yeah?" Grady said. "You should talk. You've got one yourself."

"You shut your mouth," Bradley snapped. "Don't you dare talk to me that way. I'm proud of my globe and anchor. 'Semper fi,' Forever loyal. We Marines all share that oath."

Grady hadn't been looking for a fight, and he knew he'd gone too far. Sawyer couldn't stop staring at the tattoo, with all its harsh lines and red spirals. "Is that in Japanese?" she asked. "Do you think it actually says something?"

Julie, always the peacemaker, rested her hand on Bradley's shoulder. "Grady," she said, "I'm sorry you got the tattoo the way you did, but it's done now, and we are so glad to have you home. Let's not spoil it with something we can't change. Do you have medicine for it? It looks infected."

Grady nodded. "I've been doing what the guy said. I know it doesn't look good, but it's actually a little better."

"Does it hurt?" Sawyer asked. She imagined how much it must have hurt to get it, and how much it must be hurting now.

"It's a little sore, but I can handle it," Grady grimaced.

Bradley sighed. Grady could tell he felt bad about the way he yelled. Grady felt sorry too. "Don't get me wrong, Grady – tattoos can be fine in some circumstances. They are a meaningful art form in many cultures, but what you did is way outside the scope of acceptable. Why did you do this to yourself?"

"I really don't want to talk about this anymore, maybe later, but not now." Grady needed to escape. "Is there any way to get down to that beach from here?" He pointed to the cliff and hoped Sawyer would take the hint.

"The stairs are right behind our backyard," she nodded. "It's a short walk. I'll show you the tide pools. They're right below our house," Sawyer was anxious to leave this argument behind. She saw a scary new side of Bradley, and it worried her.

"Sure, Slick," Grady, said. "Let's go."

CHAPTER 11

The Deal

The sand was especially hot on Sawyer's feet today. She still needed to spend more time barefoot to toughen them up. Grady wandered over the rocks, not wanting to slip on the wet stones. He kept his head down, looking for crabs and starfish. Sawyer admired the expanse of the ocean, which was now topped with a clear blue sky. A bank of clouds loomed on the horizon. She knew another downpour was coming. Grady turned to his new sister and watched her take it all in. He was grateful she'd helped him escape.

"Has it been tough?" Grady asked. "You know — moving from Kansas, saying goodbye, and living with my dad." Grady stooped down to check out a shell.

"Usually your dad's okay. He loves my mom and it's good to see her happy again. I really miss my grandparents, but they're coming over for Christmas. I can't wait to see them," Sawyer said.

"Have you met any of the kids on base yet?" He asked.

"No, but I met this girl Kaleʻa at school. She's nice.

I even went to a party at her house. I think we'll be friends, but I'm not so sure about the others. I'm afraid they think I'm weird. Maybe you could drive me to her house, or we could pick her up and bring her here?"

"Sure, Slick, whatever you want. I don't have any plans," Grady said.

Sawyer gave him a pat on the back. "I'm sorry about the tattoo thing, Grady. Lots of people have them over here. Kaleʻa's dad has his entire back covered and it looks really cool. Your dad will get used to it."

"He's right though, Sawyer. I should have given it a lot more thought. I don't know what all these characters mean. Ever since I got it, I've been having trouble sleeping."

"You mean it hurts too much to sleep?"

"No. I mean…" he trailed off. He wasn't sure if he wanted to admit it. "I've been having terrible nightmares. It sucks. Every time I close my eyes I see these horrible things."

"No wonder you look so awful. Are you going to tell your dad?"

"I'm not sure. I was hoping they would go away, but so far they're just getting more intense."

He hadn't talked to anyone else about the dreams. Opening up to Sawyer took a weight off his shoulders, but talking about it made them feel more real.

"I come down here when I can't sleep," Sawyer confessed. "Maybe you should, too. It's peaceful late at night. If I'm feeling lonesome or like I just need to get away from everything, I sneak out and sit on that rock at the end of the jetty."

Sawyer pointed to a lava outcropping by the shoreline. Grady shook his head. Before he met her, he thought she'd just be into ponies and princesses, but it took guts to jump from one slick rock to the next, especially in the dark. She was a better adventurer than he was.

"You come down here at night and you manage to get out to that rock?" He couldn't believe it.

"Sometimes I just need to get away from everything," Sawyer sighed. "When I'm super lonesome, I sneak out of the house, come down here, and sit out there. It really helps."

Grady knew what his dad would do if he discovered Sawyer was sneaking out to this forbidden beach in the middle of the night. "If you get caught, you"ll be grounded forever." Grady warned, "My dad doesn't approve of breaking the rules, especially on the base."

"I'm careful, and besides, nothing has happened so far," Sawyer said. She'd never give up her sanctuary, no matter what anyone said. Grady figured he should warn her it was dangerous, but he had to admire her. He nodded and let it drop. They turned in the deep sand and started back to the steps. Grady looked at Sawyer and said, "I'll keep your hideaway a secret, Slick, but you have to promise not to tell my dad about the nightmares. Deal?"

"Deal." She hid her face so he couldn't see her smile. Before they reached the top of the bluff, Sawyer turned around to face Grady, who was trudging behind her. "Now we both have something on each other," Sawyer said.

Grady chuckled. "Let's go up and see if we can arrange a day with Kale'a," he said. "I'd be glad to take you over to see her tomorrow if I can get the car."

Sawyer grabbed Grady's hand and pulled him up the last steep step.

CHAPTER 12

The Beach Trip

Jasmine handed Kale'a the sunblock and a towel warm from the dryer. "Where are you going to take Sawyer and her brother?" she asked.

"I'm not sure," Kale'a said. "It depends on Grady. We can surf, body board, or rent a kayak at the beach park from Uncle Leon." She crammed the towel into her beach bag. Jasmine kissed the top of her head as she turned and hurried toward the door.

"See you later, Mom."

"A hui hau kākau!" Jasmine waved. She could see how nervous and excited her daughter was to meet Sawyer's big brother.

"Yeah, yeah, until we meet again," Kale'a said. She skipped out to the driveway and left her mother behind her.

"Cute," Jasmine said.

Kaleʻa stood outside for what felt like forever. She couldn't wait for Sawyer and her brother to come. He sounded a lot nicer than her brother Kanoa. He didn't pay attention to her, but when he did, it was always the wrong kind. He criticized her and everything that was important to her – her sports, her school, and her friends.

He was rude to Sawyer just because she was new to the island. Kaleʻa didn't want to explain why he acted the way he did. She thought Grady must be different, because he'd agreed to take them to the beach. Her brother would never do that.

She heard the sound of the car on the gravel and knew they were coming down the drive. She waved as they came into view and grabbed her bag. When the car came to a stop, she jumped into the backseat. "Hi!" she said. Her grin wilted when she saw how worn-out Grady looked. Was something wrong with him?

"Where are we headed?" Grady asked. He stared down the road when he spoke.

"I thought we would try Kailua Beach Park," Kaleʻa suggested. "The waves may be small, but the beach is great, and the market there has the best breakfast wraps. If you want better surf, we can go to Kalamas, which is the best place to boogie board, or we could try Cockroach and longboard with some of my friends. It's a longer drive, but it's worth it." Kaleʻa sounded like the expert on waves.

"The Beach Park sounds great," Grady said. "I'm hungry, and I can't go into the water yet, so the waves don't matter. Is it far from here?"

"About fifteen minutes," Kaleʻa said. She didn't understand why he couldn't get wet. Didn't all teenagers love the water?

Kaleʻa pointed out the waterfalls that amazed Sawyer the day she arrived. "The waterfalls are cool, but they only flow when it's raining. They'll dry up by this afternoon unless we get another downpour." Grady glanced up at the mountains, but he was more focused on where they were going, not the scenery.

"Why aren't we going to a closer beach?" He kept an even tone. He didn't want to sound accusatory. Kaleʻa seemed to know her way around the island, but Grady was curious.

"Kaneohe has a bay with lots of small marinas for the boats, but Kailua has the best beach on the island," she said.

Grady nodded. "Cool."

They turned off the road at a little green market and drove past a line of old cottages to the parking area.

There were clusters of pine trees, but no water. "Where's the beach?" he asked.

"You'll see," Kaleʻa said, with her usual knowing tone. "You have to get all the way to the edge of the cliff to see the water. The trees are great for shade when it gets too hot."

As they climbed the sandy cliff, Grady was glad he'd taken Sawyer's advice and worn slippers. The tiny pinecones covering the sand would've been murder on his tender feet, though they didn't seem to bother most of the beachgoers. Grady looked back up from his feet and his mouth dropped open in awe. A cove arched from miles away at the Marine base to the coast where they stood, then at least another mile beyond. The clear water rippled aquamarine. The beaches of California paled in comparison. People walked along the shore. Dogs, wet and sandy, jumped into the surf chasing sticks and balls. Wind surfers cut through the swells and multicolored kites dotted the sky. Some children jumped in the small waves, while others were busy constructing sandcastles or deep moats just out of the water's reach. Grady smiled at Sawyer. "Some things about the military aren't so bad, are they Slick?"

Sawyer grinned back. "Guess that's true, Grady."

Kale'a headed down the beach to her favorite spot with Sawyer and Grady following behind. They spread their towels and sat down. "Is it always this breezy here?" Grady asked. "It feels great."

"Sometimes it's so windy the sand flies into your face and the waves are impossible to surf," Kale'a said. "Today is a good day." Kale'a looked out over the cove.

"See those little islands? They're called the Mokes, short for Mokeluas. We're very protective of them. Flat Island is over there That's where the surfers catch the best waves. That's Double Hump next to it, but you can't see Rabbit Island from here. We can rent a kayak and go out if you like. We can't land on them, though. They're protected, and the interior's a bird sanctuary." She finished her tour guide spiel and turned to Grady to check his reaction. She wasn't sure he'd been listening. Grady bent over to spread his towel and Kale'a reached to help him straighten it. She froze when she saw his leg. She was eye level with the tattoo and the sight of the Japanese characters made her skin crawl. Grady was gazing out at the Mokes and didn't notice the look on her face, but Sawyer did. Kale'a turned away, fiddled with her sunscreen, and mumbled, "I'm going in the water."

"I'll get some breakfast wraps and meet you both back here," Grady said as he walked away.

Sawyer found herself sitting alone. She wondered what on earth had just happened. She jumped up and jogged out to the water after Kale'a.

"What's wrong?" she asked.

"It's that tattoo," Kale'a shook her head. "Do you have any idea what it means?"

"No. Neither does Grady. He just chose it from a bunch of samples on the wall at the tattoo parlor because he liked the design."

"Well, he should have done some research!" Kale'a snapped. "I don't know what all the characters say, but I know one of them is the kanji for a noisy crow."

"Noisy crow?" Sawyer was confused. "What's so bad about that?"

"It means a lot of things – ugliness, awfulness, maybe even evil." She trailed off.

"No way!" Sawyer gasped. "Maybe that's why Grady is having nightmares."

"It's no wonder," Kale'a said.

"Is there anything he can do? I'm really worried about him. He's lost weight, he can't sleep, and he's edgy all the time. It's not like him."

"I'm surprised he can sleep at all!" Kaleʻa looked embarrassed by her outburst, but she needed to say it. "Grady's in deep trouble. I think he needs to talk to my parents. Remember, my mom teaches Japanese culture and language. She'll know what the tattoo says. Dad has lots of experience with tattoos. Maybe they can figure out what to do."

Sawyer's stomach began to somersault. They walked back to the towels and saw Grady approach with bags of food and drinks.

"What should we say?" Sawyer asked Kaleʻa, before he was close enough to hear.

"We better tell him now before it gets worse," she said.

They ate in silence. Grady finished first and complimented Kaleʻa on her choice of the beach and the food. She nodded but didn't say anything.

Finally, Sawyer stammered, "Grady, I think Kaleʻa might know why you are having nightmares. You know how you thought it might be because of the tattoo?

Well, she recognized one of those characters. It's not good."

Grady glared at Sawyer.

"You told her about the nightmares?" he shouted, "I thought we had a deal."

"I only told her after she told me what the character said. She's scared and so am I. You have to do something about it," Sawyer pleaded. "It's the noisy crow!"

"So?" Grady chuckled and tried to act casual. "It means ugly, awful! It's bad, Grady."

"How would you even know?" he said, getting defensive.

Kaleʻa shook her head. "Both my parents study Japanese, and I pay attention whenever I can. It's not so unusual to learn another language here. I know a lot of Hawaiian and some Tagalog, too," she explained.

"When you put something negative on your body, it can affect your personality, your health, and even your soul. You should've made sure you knew what the symbols meant." Kaleʻa's anger surprised him. It was more than he expected from a 12 year-old girl, but he was getting used to that. "I can't believe a tattoo artist would do something like that. Why didn't you speak up and ask what it said?"

Grady wanted to put this little girl in her place, but he knew she might be right. "So just what do you think I should do?" he shot back.

"Come to my house," she said. "Meet my parents. I think they can help you."

Grady didn't want to believe it. He was tired and beginning to lose control. "I'll be fine. Don't worry about it. You two are just overreacting." He tried to calm down.

The joy of the beach trip was gone. They picked up their towels, shook out the sand, and headed back to the car. Kaleʻa frowned as they drove up to her house. "Won't you come in, Grady?" she begged.

"Another time." Grady waited for her door to close and gunned the engine. Gravel sprayed as he backed out of the driveway. He couldn't see the pebbles hitting the back of Kaleʻa's legs.

CHAPTER 13

The Nightmare

Grady floated in the blackness of deep sleep. The black began to fade, and the heat intensified. That familiar head emerged, opened its massive jaws, and spewed a scalding shower of fire in orange, purple, and red. The flames licked around his body. He felt like he was suffocating and took a desperate gasp of air. Then the dragon reared back, its golden eyes locked onto his. At this distance, he was terrified to see not just one but multiple heads twisting in the fog. The dragon's roar left Grady's ears ringing. He scrambled to get out of the way, but a writhing tail knocked him off his feet. Grady fell in a tailspin, like a pilot out of control, the hard Earth getting closer with every second.

He woke up moaning and drenched in sweat. His body quivered. He gulped the humid air and prayed his heart would stop racing.

Sawyer cracked open the door. She crept into the room and whispered, "Grady. Grady. Are you okay?"

He couldn't answer. He just lay in bed, staring at the fan turning in lazy circles above him. Sawyer ran to the bathroom and soaked a towel with cold water, then brought it to Grady and pressed it against his forehead. She felt him jump at her touch.

"It's me, Grady. You had a nightmare, but you're awake now."

He raised his eyes and looked at her, trying to re-enter reality. "I'm so tired," he sighed, "but I'm afraid to sleep. The images get worse each time." He squinted remembering the dragon, and he was sure it was a dragon now. Its eyes haunted him. "It's evil," he shuddered. "I don't know what to do."

"Maybe I should call Kale'a," Sawyer offered. "Her parents are really nice. Wouldn't it be worth it to at least give it a try?"

Grady rose up on one elbow and stared at Sawyer. He looked so forlorn she fought back tears. She had to stay calm. Crying would only make things worse.

All Grady could manage was, "Okay, do it," before he collapsed and threw an arm over his face.

Sawyer locked her fingers in his outstretched hand and squeezed. She watched his breathing slow and his face relax. "I'll arrange a visit," she said. "You just close your eyes and rest until I come back."

Sawyer unlaced her fingers and backed out of the room to call Kaleʻa. Grady curled up on his side but tried not to close his eyes. He was afraid the dragon would return if he dozed off. When Sawyer finished making the arrangements, she opened the door and found Grady, knees to his chest, arms cradling his head, his eyes shut tight. She touched the crease in his forehead, wishing it away. His eyes shot open and he lurched back.

"Shh, it's only me," she said. "I let you sleep for a while, but now you need to get up, take a shower, and get dressed. We're due at Kaleʻa's house in an hour. Your dad said we could drop him at the squadron and take the car. Mom went to the beach for the afternoon."

"Did you tell them about the nightmares?" Grady voice was strained.

"No, but they know something serious is bothering you. You can't hide that," Sawyer said.

"I guess I must seem a little off," Grady admitted. "To say the least!" Sawyer helped Grady up and led him to the bathroom.

"I'll pour you some pineapple juice and make some toast," she said.

"How about some coffee?" Grady asked as she walked toward the kitchen.

Grady soaked a wash cloth with cold water and pressed it against his face. He rubbed it along the back of his neck and looked into the mirror. He was shocked by his reflection. With trembling hands, he uncapped the toothpaste and managed to brush his teeth. The minty favor was refreshing. He ran his fingers through his hair, took one last look in the mirror, shrugged, and shuffled toward the kitchen. Bradley looked up from his paper and tried to make eye contact with his son. Grady sat, bent his head, and gripped his coffee cup with both hands. He seemed unaware of his father's probing eyes.

Bradley wanted to drill him, but he wasn't sure how far to push for answers. Was it the move again, the new family situation, or his future? He was afraid he'd say the wrong thing, so he just asked, "You okay Grady?

Anything I can do?"

"Not now, Dad, but maybe we can sit down later." Grady's tone was dismissive.

"Sure, when you're ready."

Grady could hear the concern and disappointment in his father's voice, but he let the silence fill the room.

CHAPTER 14

The Explanation

Sawyer grabbed the knocker on Kaleʻaʻs door before she saw it, but jolted back when she took it in. It was in the shape of a bronze octopus, its tentacles spread, its volleyball eyes staring down at them. She reached up, her heart beating a little too fast, and gave its beak three cautious taps. Kaleʻa opened the door with an anxious look. "Come in," she said. Grady fumbled to take off his shoes and stumbled inside. He was still getting accustomed to Hawaiian traditions. A teenage boy lurked in the hallway, but at the sign of visitors, he turned into a room and shut the door behind him. "That's my brother," Kaleʻa explained . "He's not very friendly."

Grady followed her to the sofa and stood awkwardly as Kaleʻa introduced her parents. His eyes darted to the dragon sculpture that stood under the painting of a woman on the beach. A chill ran up his spine. "Grady, meet my mom and dad, Jasmine and Charlie. Mom and Dad, this is Grady." "Aloha," Charlie said.

"E komo mai." Jasmine added and gave Grady a tight hug, which he took with his arms at his sides. "Welcome to our home," she said, and waved for everyone to sit down. Grady nodded politely and sank down to the edge of the seat. He took shallow breaths and tried to stop his hands from clenching into fists. He couldn't keep his eyes off the dragon sculpture.

Kale'a scurried into the kitchen and came back with a tray. She passed out tea and set a plate of papaya, mangos, and nuts on the coffee table. Grady and Sawyer shared a look, but they both declined the food. Neither had the stomach for pūpūs. Sawyer was relieved Grady had decided to get help, but it wasn't going to be easy to explain their situation. Grady sighed and shook his head. He didn't want to relive the experience, but he felt he had no choice.

"Take your time, Grady," Charlie told him. He put a piece of mango on a small plate and handed it to Grady. Grady took the plate and gave Charlie a grateful nod, but he still couldn't bring himself to eat.

"Start at the beginning," Charlie said. "We'll want to know how this all came about."

"Okay." He cleared his throat. "So, I was done with school. I wasn't a good student. I never got into it like some kids. I couldn't believe it when my dad agreed to let me go on a road trip as a reward." He cringed at the memory. "I wanted to prove I could handle it." He trailed off, staring at the mango on his plate.

"He left right after the wedding." Sawyer gave Grady a playful flick on the ear.

Grady broke out of his thoughts with a gasp. "What was that for?"

"That's for leaving me with the lovebirds," Sawyer groaned. Grady shook his head, but her interruption broke some of the tension, and he found the heart to continue.

"My buddy Vic and I made it all the way to San Diego and met a couple of surfers named Chad and Len. Everyone wanted to party and I had heard about this club that was easy on IDs. We decided to check it out, but my directions sucked and we got totally lost. The guys were bummed and I felt like a big loser."

"Go on," Charlie said. He knit his brow and reached out to Grady. He remembered feeling like a loser too, but the last thing he wanted at that age was a stranger's pity. He grabbed a handful of nuts instead of Grady's shoulder and tossed them into his mouth.

"We were walking down this creepy street and the only light was coming from this strange antique weapons store, so we went in to find out where we'd gone wrong. The guy laughed and told us the club we were looking for had been shut down. The night turned into a disaster and it was all my fault." Grady stopped and took a sip of tea. Jasmine slid his plate a few inches closer to him with her finger, but he didn't seem to notice. Grady looked up and went on.

"When we tried to leave, this guy started in about me getting a tattoo. Chad and Len thought that was a great idea. Even Vic was all for it. And so I thought, okay, so I get some tattoo and maybe I can salvage the night and my reputation." He cleared his throat again and considered how to finish his story. "Lots of people have tattoos now, you know, so what's the big deal? Even my dad has one," he said, in his own defense.

Sawyer nodded in agreement and said, "That's right! He has that globe and anchor on his arm."

"Yeah," Grady muttered. "Semper fi. Anyway, the guy tells me to pick one off this wall of tattoo samples. I didn't want a skull, or some eagle, and I sure didn't want any Latin motto like my dad, so I went with the flames.

I figured they would be, like, the fire inside me or something." Grady rubbed his face. The shame hurt as much as the needles.

"Getting it was awful, but my buddies ate it up and I was back in their good graces. We made it to Chad and Len's apartment in O.B. a little before dawn and I crashed on the living room couch. The pain woke me up every time I moved so I didn't get much sleep. That's when I had the first nightmare." He closed his eyes and let himself remember for a second.

"I was spiraling in and out of darkness and fog. Huge jaws were coming at me, breathing fire, and a forked tongue went for my eyes. I woke up totally freaked out and decided it was time to come home." Grady leaned back on the sofa. Charlie's eyes filled with sympathy as he focused in on Grady. Jasmine held onto the tips of Charlie's fingers with the same look of concern.

"I thought being with my family would stop the nightmares, but they've only become more vivid. Each time it happens I see the monster in better detail and the dream is more intense. The jaws, the eyes, the teeth, the heat, the fire, the forked tongue..." He shivered and worked his way out of the nightmare again. "But this morning was even worse. It started with the same darkness and fog. The mouth was so close I could smell the stench of rotten flesh. Then it reared back so I could see what it was. It was a dragon with a bunch of heads, all coming for me. He lashed out at me with his tail, and I spun down into the dark fog until I woke up retching." Grady's shoulders shook. He forced down a sob and leaned into Sawyer, who clutched his clammy palm.

"Can a nightmare destroy you?" He murmured as he reached up to wipe his eyes.

Jasmine rushed over and put her arms around both of them. "No, no, don't think that. We'll find a way to make it go away. Trust me, Grady. There has to be a way."

She squeezed his hand and he squeezed back.

Kale'a held back tears, not wanting Grady to see her cry. Charlie joined Jasmine and gave Grady a pat on the back.

"That's quite an ordeal you've been through. It takes courage to admit you need help. You're not alone now. Remember that."

Grady calmed down so Jasmine and Charlie rose and went to the kitchen for more drinks. Kale'a knew they were discussing what to do. She hoped they had a solution in mind. They returned with a frosty pitcher and offered refills.

"May I see this tattoo more closely?" Jasmine knelt in front of Grady.

Grady stood and turned, so she was eye-level with his leg. She leaned forward and studied the tattoo for a long time.

She went over each detail, mouthing notes to herself, nodding and grimacing as she examined each of the four characters.

"These characters spell a name, Susanoo, and the name tells an ancient story," she said. "The first one, 'Su,' means origin, or base. Susanoo was a prince among the gods, so his base is good and solid. The second part of his name, 'sa,' includes the symbol for a plate, which means privilege, you know, like everything was handed to him on a silver platter. The third is 'no,' and that's where the problem comes – this is the one you recognized, isn't it, Kale'a?"

Kale'a blushed. She was proud that her mother knew she paid attention to the Japanese lessons.

"That's the character for the noisy crow," Jasmine continued. "It represents ugliness, the potential for evil. The last character is the symbol for Susanoo's father Mikoto, the King of the Spirits. His name means universal respect. There are many gods in the Shinto religion, and Susanoo is the God of Storms and Chaos.

His name is the story of his struggle. Do you see the flames swirling around the writing?" She pointed it out to Grady and he nodded, imagining the dragon's breath. "There are many stories of Susanoo and many versions of his myth, but the message is the same. It goes something like this: Susanoo once lived with his sister Amaterasu, the Goddess of the Sun, until one day he got angry and restless. He burned her rice fields and killed her servants in a fit of rage, and she hid herself in a cave to grieve. After the other gods persuaded Amaterasu to leave her isolation and bring light back into the world, they banished Susanoo from Heaven."

Jasmine looked up at Grady. "Your life is in turmoil," she said. "Like Susanoo, you must find a way to deal with the consequences of your decisions." She took his hand in hers and said, "You'll have to do the research yourself. When you find out how the myth ends, you'll know how it fits into your own journey. Be vigilant. You will be tested."

Jasmine moved her finger to a flame in the shape of an arrow at the bottom of the tattoo. "Here's a clue that

might help," she said.

Charlie nodded. He helped her up and stood next to his wife, supporting her with his hand on her waist.

"She's right," he agreed. "Do you understand what she's trying to tell you?"

Grady thought about it, but he was too tired to open up. He'd just met these people, and he felt like he was drowning in advice. "I don't know," he said. "I guess I messed up." He raised his eyes to Kale'a's father, and then glanced away again.

Charlie stepped towards him and clasped Grady's shoulder. "She's trying to tell you you've got an opportunity. You can learn from this, and become a better man. You can take this image on your leg and change it into something that represents you."

"But how do I do that?" Grady asked.

Charlie ran a hand through his stubbly grey hair and reflected. "I wanted to tell the story of my struggle to find a place in this world. I worked with an artist to design the tattoo on my back. He spent a long time getting to know me, and then he helped me tell my story. Many Hawaiians adopt an animal spirit. It's called our 'aumakua. It represents our family and our lineage. My line is the octopus."

Then he pulled off his shirt to show Grady his tattoo.

An octopus sat at center of his back in the middle of a tidal wave, its tentacles spread out over his back muscles. One tentacle grasped a dagger. Another held a bonsai'd cypress tree. The third cradled a child. The forth was strangling a shark. The fifth curled downward to clutch a plumeria flower. The sixth curved from his back under his arm to touch the outstretched fingertip of a hand tattooed on his shoulder. The seventh and eighth tentacles were knotted together. Grady didn't know what any of them meant, but something about the child stuck out to him.

"Is that Kale'a?" he asked. Charlie was touched by Grady's question. His eyes softened as he looked to his daughter and thought about their long journey together.

"Very good," he said. "She was born with the umbilical cord around her neck. We almost lost her that first night. She's a fighter, though and survived against all odds." He beamed at Kale'a. It looked like she'd heard the story a million times.

"I'm curious about the knot, too," Grady said. "Ah, the knot. That represents marriage. Tying the knot changes your life forever." He glanced at his wife with an affectionate smile.

"It took over a year of sessions to complete the tattoo," he continued. "The artist and I became good friends during our hours together. I'd like you to meet him. Dodge has a lot of experience with altering tattoos. As you've discovered, sometimes people get them without much thought. Some people get a tattoo when they're young, but it doesn't reflect who they've become. Your path isn't clear yet. If you want to remove it, Dodge will refer you to a professional who can do that. If you want to complete it, Dodge will help you himself. It's your decision."

"I'll give it a lot of thought," Grady said. "I promise." Sawyer could tell he meant it.

"Pomaika'i," Charlie said. "Good luck."

CHAPTER 15

The Librarian

Grady and Sawyer headed back to the military base. As they crossed over the emerald lagoon, Grady reached over, tugged her ear and said, "Thanks for making me go."

Sawyer nodded, but she couldn't manage a smile. "What are you going to do?" she asked. Her throat was tight. "What if you have another nightmare tonight?

Where are you going to find out about Susanoo and the end of the myth?"

"I feel a little better just knowing that there's an answer somewhere. I bet we can Google it."

"Pull over and take out your cell phone, Grady. We can do it right here," Sawyer said.

"Can't, Slick. I forgot to charge it last night. I don't want to go back to the house. If Dad and Julie are there,

I'll have to answer a bunch of questions. Let's keep this between you and me until we have the whole picture. There must be some place on base we can do the research. If not, we can drive to Kailua and find an Internet café."

They pulled up to the gate, where the Marine on-duty reached out to examine their IDs. Grady handed them over and asked, "Where can I do some research on base?"

The guard seemed sidetracked as he looked over their information. "The library's about a half-mile from here. You got a piece of paper?" Grady grabbed a receipt from the ashtray and handed it over for the guard to jot down directions. When they arrived at the Quonset hut, Grady's hope deflated. The domed corrugated metal building was left over from World War II. It looked more like an old garage than a hub for the worldwide web.

The door was open and a young woman in a lavender sundress sat at a table in the far corner of the room. A rotating fan barely made a dent in the heat that radiated from the metal roof. Grady and Sawyer felt like they'd stepped into an oven, but the girl seemed comfortable and content. Since no one else was there, they figured she must be in charge.

"Excuse me," Grady stammered. "Maybe you can help us? We were told that you have computers for dependents to use." Grady stared at the girl. Her blonde hair was pulled back in a ponytail and her blue eyes sparkled. Freckles were smattered across her nose.

Grady thought she had a certain grace about her, in the way she moved her hands as she paged through a surf magazine.

She glanced up and smiled. "What makes you think we have that kind of technology here?"

"Just hoping." Grady returned her smile.

Sawyer silently watched the exchange with a mix of fascination and alarm. Were they flirting? How could he flirt at a time like this? She gave a little snort and added, "Do you have a history section? Maybe we can find a book on myths and legends."

The girl turned her gaze to Sawyer. "Sure, over there," she said. Her ponytail swung as she jerked her head to the right. "The last row is our history section."

They looked over the sparse collection of books and knew they'd never find anything on Susanoo here.

Grady and Sawyer shared a look of dismay and turned to the girl with apologetic frowns. "Sorry for wasting your time," Grady sighed.

"We have access to the other libraries on the islands," the girl offered. "Maybe I can order the book you need."

Grady and Sawyer nodded, then Grady turned his attention back to the girl.

"I appreciate your help," he said. "By the way, I'm Grady, and this is my sister, Sawyer. My dad was just stationed here."

"I'm Chloe. My dad's been here for about a year. I'm home for the summer. Good duty station, isn't it?"

Sawyer barely heard Chloe's response. That was the first time Grady had ever called her sister instead of Slick. Her skin tingled and her face flushed red. She smiled at Grady who was focusing on the computer screen.

Chloe pressed the "on" button and the computer came to life. She accessed the Hawaiian Library's site and Grady sat down and watched as she typed in "Susanoo," but the computer didn't find any matches. Grady sighed and started to get up.

"Maybe you were too specific," Sawyer suggested.

"Try searching Japanese mythology."

The computer took forever before a short list of books popped up on screen. Grady frowned as they read through the offerings. There were no listings for Susanoo, but another book caught his attention: "Japanese Gods and Goddesses and Their Place in Japanese Culture." It was located on Lānai at the Cultural History Library.

"Can you order this one for me?" Grady didn't want to sound too enthusiastic, but he couldn't help it.

"Sure. It will take a couple of weeks though."

Grady's shoulders slumped. "Is there any way to make it faster? This is really important."

"You're in Hawaii," Chloe frowned. "Things take time here. Maybe you should look it up on the Internet. The Internet Café next to the Exchange is open twenty four hours." She looked over her guests again. What was Grady's hurry? She couldn't figure out what could be so urgent about some old mythology books.

"Good idea!" Grady wondered why the guard hadn't sent them there in the first place. He stood and turned to leave. "Come on, Slick. Let's head over to the Exchange."

"Wait," Chloe murmured. "We aren't supposed to use this computer for personal stuff, but I guess I could claim we were looking up decorations for the base's summer luau or something." She took her seat, entered her password, and typed "Susanoo." They scanned through a list of sites, and Grady's face went white when he saw the words, "Susanoo and The Legend of the Eight-Headed Dragon."

His nightmares came flashing back, the mouths, the tongues, and the fire. "That's it!" He turned to Sawyer and whispered, "That dragon was in my nightmare."

Sawyer nodded. She was excited they were finally getting somewhere. "Chloe, can you go to that link?"

Susanoo's wild hair and long beard fanned around him. His mouth was wide open in a scream and his eyes filled with terror as he stared down a dragon sporting eight heads and eight tails. There were Japanese characters in corner of the page, familiar but impossible to read. A couple of paragraphs describing the myth sat under the image of Susanoo. His heart thumping, Grady asked Chloe to print the page.

"What's this all about?" she asked.

"It's a long story for another time," Grady said. "Thank you for all your help. I'd like to come back and fill you in, if you're really interested."

"Why not?" Chloe handed them the printout.

Grady and Sawyer walked out and gave each other a high five as they climbed in the car. "That was almost a wild goose chase," Grady said. "I guess I should've been clearer with the gate guard, but then we might not have ended up at the library. It had a few things going for it." Grady commented.

Sawyer rolled her eyes. "You mean the charming Chloe?"

Grady had that twinkle in his eye, but he changed the subject. "Let's get the car back to the house and go down to the beach. We can take some time and read this in private. It'll be tough to wait, but we were due back an hour ago, and there's no use getting busted now. We'll need to use the car again soon."

CHAPTER 16

The Myth

The water washed over the rocks and Grady and Sawyer's bare feet. They sat on the lava outcropping, bent over the picture of Susanoo. Grady read from the text, "Susanoo was banished from the heavens. In a state of unrest and turmoil, he created storms and chaos over the earth until he came to a simple village, where he met an old couple weeping over their daughter. When he asked what was wrong, they said they used to have eight daughters until the terrible dragon Orochi demanded he eat one each year. Now only one daughter remained. Susanoo faced Orochi, the beast with eight heads and eight tails. The dragon sprayed him with flames and clawed Susanoo's face as his eight tails whipped from side to side, preventing his escape." Grady stopped reading and looked out at the ocean.

"These are the images in my nightmares. I never get past this part because everything turns black. I always fall into the darkness screaming and then wake up." "Then it's even more important to finish the myth. If Susanoo can defeat the dragon, maybe it will be the clue we need to help you," Sawyer offered.

"But what if he doesn't win? The odds are so great against him. He has no weapons to battle a towering dragon with eight heads and tails no less."

"Maybe he's clever instead of strong. I bet I could outwit a dragon."

Grady laughed. "I don't know, Sawyer. If he has eight heads, doesn't he have eight brains?"

"Nah," Sawyer shook her head. "It's got to be dumb.

I bet it only has one brain split into eight pieces!" "Maybe," Grady shrugged. "Or maybe it's Susanoo that gets cut into pieces and roasted for dinner!"

Sawyer rolled her eyes at Grady's comment, grabbed the computer printout, and continued to read silently.

Then she sighed and handed the paper back to him. "Well, is Susanoo toast?" Grady asked. He raised his eyebrows. He was embarrassed to be so caught up in the fantasy. "Or does he figure out a way to slay the dragon?"

"Read it yourself," Sawyer said.

Grady mouthed the words as he started reading to himself, then he shook his head and sighed. "I need to read this out loud or it's not gonna stick." He straightened the printout and started again.

"In search of a weapon and desperate to protect himself, Susanoo grabbed one of the beast's eight tails. It stiffened in

97

his grasp, and he realized he could plunge the pointed tip into the dragon's heart. Susanoo darted from side to side until he pierced the soft tissue of its bulging breast. The dragon lurched backward as the sword pierced his scaly hide. He reared up to come at Susanoo again, but the fire from his great jaws flickered out. He staggered only once before he fell to the ground with a pitiful groan. Susanoo's first reward was his life, but the greatest reward was saving the princess, who became his wife. Finally, his act of courage satisfied the

gods who granted him salvation. He and his princess lived through eternity, together in peace."

Grady stared at the picture of Susanoo. "My dragons are inside my head, and much more difficult to identify and conquer."

"At least you can admit it," Sawyer offered. "But you know, the story of Susanoo doesn't exactly match yours. He was awful to his sister but you've always been great to me."

"You didn't think so when I was using my wrestling moves on you," he reminded her.

"True, but it's not like burning fields and killing servants."

"You're being too literal, Slick."

"Yeah, I get that it's a myth, and this is real life," she agreed, "but what do you call the nightmares?

Grady's mouth hung open for a moment. "Wake up calls?" he offered.

Sawyer nodded and stuck her nose in the air. "We all have dragons to battle. Some are tougher than others." Grady took it in, impressed she understood so well. "What? You surprised how smart I am?" Grady pulled a slimy piece of seaweed from the top of the rock and tossed it onto Sawyer's lap. "Eww, Grady!" Sawyer shrieked. She threw it back at him, and he let it slide off the rock and back into the ocean.

"I'll keep that in mind," Grady said. "Do you think there's a princess in my future too, or is that just part of the myth?"

"Absolutely!" she laughed.

He pictured Chloe and said, "Hope you're right."

Grady and Sawyer wandered up the stairs from the beach and took the winding path to their house. Both were absorbed by the information they had just read. Sawyer opened the screen door and the aroma of chicken potpie hit her. For a moment she thought she was back at the farmhouse watching Gran make her favorite dish. A wave of homesickness enveloped her, but she knew it would destroy her mom if she broke down. "Wow, Mom," she said, keeping her voice from cracking. "You made Gran's favorite recipe."

Julie beamed. "Yes, and we're having corn on the cob, cucumber salad and chilled watermelon for dessert."

"Why don't the two of you wash up and set up the picnic table out on the porch?" Bradley said. "We'll eat in ten minutes."

It only took two bites of potpie before Bradley started his interrogation. "So where did you two go today after you dropped me off?"

Grady was quick to answer, "You have my cell number in case of an emergency. I don't see why you need to know exactly where I've gone."

Julie gave Grady a stern look, "When you have Sawyer with you, we need to know where you're going, especially when your cell phone is here on the charger."

Grady backed off, but he was clearly angry about the confrontation. He started to stand, ready to escape, when Sawyer put her hand on his arm. She didn't want Bradley to get too worked up. "Just tell them," she said. "We have a plan now, and you should share it on your own terms."

Grady played with his dinner and ate a bite of corn. Then he let out a deep sigh and started with the nightmares, the meeting with Kale'a's parents, and the trip to the library, the information they'd found, and finally the proposed trip to the tattoo studio. By the time he was done, the food was cold and the lemonade was warm.

"Go ahead and say it, Dad. You told me I wasn't ready for a tattoo."

Bradley put down his napkin and looked Grady in the eye. "I agree with you about the tattoo, but I'm proud of both of you for finding a way to deal with it."

Grady was shocked at the response while Sawyer blushed with pleasure. Bradley held up his hand and continued. "But from this point forward Julie, and I have to be involved. We love you Grady and when you suffer, we suffer, too. Please trust us to help you in any way we can."

"Okay, Dad. When we get back tomorrow we'll fill you in. Can we borrow the car again?" Grady pressed his luck.

"Only if your cell phone is charged and with you." Julie shook her spoon at Grady.

"Can we nuke the dinner, Mom?" Sawyer asked, bringing everyone back to the dinner table. "I'm hungry and I've been looking forward to Gran's potpie ever since we got home."

"Good idea," Julie said. "Let's start dinner over on a better note." Sawyer and her mom gathered the plates and went into the kitchen as Grady and his father watched each other in silence.

Finally Grady said, "Dad, thanks for listening and not making me feel worse than I do."

"We all make bad decisions, son. What's important is how we correct them and what we learn from the experience." Bradley gave his son a long look. He could see how much Grady wanted to make him proud. He held out his hand and Grady took it with a grin.

CHAPTER 17

Koi Tattoo

The trip to Dodge's tattoo studio in Kailua took
about twenty minutes. Grady and Charlie chatted in
the front seat while Sawyer was unusually quiet in the
back. Grady's driving challenged the patience of Hawaii's
typically courteous drivers. He was blissfully unaware of
his shortcomings as they waved him onto roads, through
stop signs, and onto busy streets. Charlie acknowledged
each courteous gesture with an apologetic gesture of his
own. He breathed a sigh of relief when they parked on a
side street. Charlie was grateful to stand and stretch his
sea legs.

The busy downtown reminded Sawyer of Colby. The
buildings were newer here, but it had the same small town
charm. It wasn't a tourist trap, that's for sure.

Colby might've been a little more vintage, but Kailua felt familiar to her. Charlie led the way to Koi Tattoo, sandwiched in a row of businesses. Dodge's shop was halfway down, next to a restaurant called Island Chow. The smell of homemade barbecue ribs filled the air and caused another wave of homesickness to overcome Sawyer. She had no idea what to expect and worried it would be some seedy tattoo parlor with beaded doorways and menacing figures on the wall. They opened the glass front door into a clean and cheery atmosphere.

Dodge sat beside a tall counter, working in a sketchbook. He seemed oblivious to his visitors. A colorful mural of a dragon extended from one end of the back wall to the other. It had one head, wasn't breathing fire, and was far less menacing than the dragon in Grady's dreams. This one spread its majestic wings outward, showcasing the brilliant green scales that covered its body. The other walls were decorated with pen and ink drawings, oil paintings, and watercolors. Sculptures of gurus, gods, and Buddhas rested on the bookshelves. Sawyer's eyes were drawn to an aquarium filled with brightly colored fish.

"Wow," she said. "Look at those neon colors!" Grady turned to look and remembered the aquarium filled with tarantulas in O.B.

Dodge looked up from his sketchbook. "Did you notice the two salamanders?" He went over to the tank and dipped his hand under the water. "Salamanders are very Zen," he glanced at Sawyer, to see if she was still into it. "This is Richard. He likes to be petted." Dodge stroked the creature with his index finger. "Tommy's the big bully." Dodge eased Richard back into the water. "He likes to chomp on fingers." Dodge's brown eyes flashed as he grinned. He had a shaved head and a tidy gray-streaked goatee. His body was a canvas, one scene blending into the next, each a part of Dodge's journey through life.

"Hey Charlie, good to see you. How's the family?" "Pretty good, Dodge. How about you?"

"Kids are great. Pippy is chattering in Hawaiian, English, and her own gibberish. Her favorite word is still pau."

"Pow?" Sawyer laughed.

"It was her first word. It's Hawaiian for done or finished. She used to push her plate away and try to get out of her high chair while saying 'pau.' She's convinced we understand everything and will obey her every wish." Dodge laughed enjoying telling the story. "Peggy's first birthday is Saturday. We're doing an Imu pig in the backyard. We hope your family will come."

"Sounds great," Charlie said. "Dodge, this is Grady and his sister, Sawyer. I told you a little about his tattoo."

Dodge nodded a greeting to them both. "So what's up with this tattoo you got?" He asked.

Grady started with the road trip and tried not to leave anything out. When he began to explain the myth of Susanoo and the dragon, Dodge shook his head in dismay. When he finished, Dodge looked into his eyes and asked, "So what have you learned from this experience?"

Grady didn't know what to say. He looked to Sawyer, then to Charlie, and back to Dodge. "I just wanted to be one of the guys. We've moved so many times. It seems like

I'm always starting over, trying to fit into new schools, new neighborhoods, new towns, trying to figure out who's willing to accept an outsider like me." Grady ran his hand over his tattoo.

"Yeah, it sucks, doesn't it?" Dodge said.

Grady laughed and shook his head. "They've grown up together," he said. "They have so many in-jokes and secrets. I'm always the odd man out. Sometimes it gets so lonely. I know I shouldn't have done it, but we had some beers and the guys were egging me on, so I just did. It was a huge mistake, and I'm not sure how to fix it."

Sawyer wanted to reach out and touch Grady as he told his story, but she stood still. She was caught in her own fears about her new life and what moving had meant to her. This was only the beginning. She would have to face years of the same loneliness Grady went through.

"At least you know you made a mistake and you want to fix it," Dodge said. "That's a good beginning. Let me take a look at the work the last guy did. I need to see how deep he went, especially with the red." Dodge had Grady put his leg up on the sofa and bent down to get a better look. He put on a latex glove, ran his hand over the tattoo, and pulled at the skin. Grady winced.

"Sorry," Dodge said. "I can give you a couple of options.

You could have the tattoo removed. There's a doctor in town that will do it, but it'll be painful and it won't be cheap. There will still be traces of red ink from the flames, even if you get it lasered off. It can't be helped."

Grady looked conflicted, "Exactly how much is that gonna hurt?" he asked.

"More than it did to get it," Dodge admitted. He gave him something between a grimace and a smile. "If you don't want to get it removed, I often rework tattoos for people. I can give you something that better represents who you are at this stage of your life. Many people who get tattoos early in their lives no longer find them so important, and they want to take them off their bodies. Others add to their tattoos as they mature and conquer their problems. You're pretty young to have a tattoo like that, and I know you didn't put much thought into it.

Maybe that's why it's causing you problems. Only you can decide what's right for you."

Grady sighed. "What would you recommend? I can't go on like this."

"I'm not going to make that choice for you, but I will need to get to know you better if you choose to change the tattoo and you want me to do the work. I'll also give you the card of the doctor who can remove it. Take the time to think this through, then give me a call and we'll talk some more. I'm sure we can work together to find a solution."

Grady got up and shook Dodge's hand. "Thanks. I'll think about it, and make a decision soon. I don't want to have these nightmares anymore. I'm afraid the myth will take me over."

Dodge nodded. "We want to layer your story over the myth, just like we can lay it over your tattoo."

As they were walking out the door, Dodge called out to Charlie, "Hey, why don't you bring Grady and his family to Peggy's luau on Saturday? It'll give them a chance to meet my 'ohana, and I can spend a little more time with Grady."

Charlie looked over at Grady and Sawyer. "Sounds good," Grady said. He walked out the door and then poked his head back in a second later. "By the way, what does 'ohana mean?"

"It means family. 'Ohana is the center of life. Right, Charlie?"

Charlie grinned, thinking of his own family. "Always," he said.

CHAPTER 18

Car Ride Revelations

As soon as they got in the car, Sawyer started asking questions.

"How did you meet Dodge? Why did he become a tattoo artist?" she burst out.

Charlie buckled into the passenger side of the car, hoping the ride back would be less bumpy than the first. "I met him out at the marina one day. He tattooed a guy in trade for a small fishing boat. Dodge was trying to launch it, but he was having trouble with the motor stalling, so I helped him get it going and we started talking about fishing. It was good for me to meet a haole with the proper respect for the Hawaiian ways."

"A haole?" Grady repeated the strange term. His dad used it when he talked about the way Hawaiians treated the military here.

"It's Hawaiian slang for white people or foreigners like you. The term used to refer to any outsider in the Hawaiian kingdoms before explorers like Captain Cook arrived, but usually it refers to the bad experiences Hawaiians have had with white men." Charlie put his thumb to his lips and chewed his nail. He wasn't sure how much he wanted to tell them.

"You mean like the missionaries?" Sawyer asked. "We studied them in school last year."

"That's part of it," Charlie nodded. "Traders and missionaries came came to exchange goods and bring us their religion. In the beginning, they helped the King, but in time, they wanted us to be more like them. They insisted on changing our culture." Charlie sighed, and decided to go ahead and tell the real story. "When King Kamehameha died and his two sons inherited it all, they allowed the first foreigners to buy land in Kaneohe.

Later, Queen Kalama partnered with an American named Harris to establish the Kaneohe Sugar Company. More foreign advisors bought land and invested in sugar.

When she died, the land passed out of Hawaiian hands to them. They hired foreign workers, mostly from Asia, to work with Hawaiians in the fields and to live in villages on the plantations. Sugar stopped turning a profit, so they turned the land into cattle ranches and housing developments. The workers lost their jobs and their homes. The grazing cattle destroyed the natural vegetation and ruined the land."

Charlie closed his eyes, trying to picture the countryside as he'd seen it when he was a child. "I remember visiting my great-grandfather when I was a little keiki and he lived at Kaneohe village. We would walk hand- in-hand in his little garden. It had taro, sweet potatoes, breadfruit and bananas for the family." Charlie tried not to let his bottom lip shake. "He lost all of it. That's why we're fishermen now. No one can own the ocean." "That's awful," Grady said. He frowned and stared blankly ahead, lost in thought as the red light turned to green. The cars behind him started honking and Charlie pointed up at the signal. Grady's face went red and he floored it. "But why don't Hawaiians like the military either?" he asked, trying to restore the balance. "What did they do?"

Charlie took his time before answering. He gripped the shoulder strap of his seatbelt. "Well, the military was worried about a Japanese invasion even before World War II. They dredged the Kaneohe Bay reefs to develop the area for the Naval Station at Mokapu which is now Kaneohe Marine Base." He sighed. "Not only did they change our bay and beaches, but they took advantage of our hospitality while letting off steam in Honolulu." Charlie shook his head as he recalled too many stories of servicemen and their wild parties. "After the war, the government wanted more tourists to boost the economy. Now they're all over, expecting little grass shacks and hula girls. They just stroll our streets with their heads in their phones or behind their cameras. They have no concern for traffic and it's our responsibility not to run them over."

"I had no idea, Charlie. I'm so sorry." Grady was sad and embarrassed by what he heard. He wondered if he'd ever acted like a haole without realizing it. He'd been guilty of walking around staring at his text messages before.

Charlie let go of his seatbelt and eased back into his seat. "It wasn't all bad. Without the Filipino workers, Jasmine's family wouldn't be here," he grinned, "and we wouldn't have fallen in love. Now that would be terrible." He gave a final nod and finished his story. "Hawaii is a true melting pot, and we've learned to get along pretty well."

It dawned on Sawyer that Kaleʻa's brother Kanoa grew up with this history. She could understand why he treated her and Grady like haoles, but he wasn't very nice to his own sister either. Maybe it was an unfortunate mix of prejudice and sibling rivalry. Sawyer decided that she wouldn't let him bother her. In fact, she was going to make a point of treating him extra nice the next time she saw him. Maybe that would soften his opinion a bit.

"Dodge was different," Charlie continued. "He took the time to research before he started fishing. He learned how to catch live bait, how to cast, which fish to release and which ones to eat. He was open to the Hawaiian culture and so we became friends." Charlie grabbed the dashboard as Grady turned a corner. He winced and his knuckles went white. "We would go out to the Mokes in the boat or on kayaks to fish and dive. One day, he paddled out on his own and his kayak went under. He was on the far side of the islands where the sea is roughest. There's no shore there, only steep cliffs. He almost drowned getting to a jagged ledge where he could catch his breath and climb to safety."

Grady remembered stories his dad would tell of pilots ejecting from their jets over water to wait for rescue. His eyes darted from the road to Charlie.

"Watch the road, Grady!" Charlie pointed as he spoke. Grady swerved to avoid a loose dog. Charlie looked desperate to get out of the car, but he took a deep breath and went on. "Dodge worried he'd never get back to shore. He thought he'd never see his kids grow up."

"That must have been so scary," Sawyer said under her breath.

"The experience affected him deeply. Dodge believes we're all connected. I'm sure he thinks that you appeared in his shop for some greater purpose. It's an intriguing philosophy, don't you think?" Charlie watched Grady as he took it all in.

Grady considered what Charlie said. "If he's right about being connected, it could be an important part of my journey. Sawyer's too. Maybe even his."

Charlie nodded.

"I wish Dodge had done my tattoo," Grady said. His shoulders slumped and his mind left the road again.

"You're under age so he would've turned you down.

If he does agree now, it will be because he knows you well and can design a piece of art that truly reflects who you are and who want to become."

Grady braked hard to avoid a car that shot into his lane. Charlie lurched forward, then pulled himself back and braced himself for impact. Grady gave a short honk and the tires squealed as they barely missed colliding with the car. "Oops," Grady muttered.

Charlie's stomach churned. Grady tried to change the subject. "So, I didn't see any samples on the walls. Does he keep them in a book?"

Charlie cleared his throat, found his voice, and said, "Each piece is an original. No copies, just one of a kind. He has an album that shows the quality of his work, but he never repeats a design."

Sawyer considered her own life and tried to come up with an image that she'd want on her body. Maybe something to do with sports like a soccer ball, or a stalk of wheat to remind her of home, or even a portrait of Gaboochie. The more she thought about it, the more obvious it became that she'd need to wait a long time before she was ready.

Charlie squinted as the car swerved around the winding road. "My nephew Sammy wanted a guardian angel on his shoulder in honor of his mother. He brought in a Christmas card and asked if Dodge could copy the angel on it." Charlie chuckled. He couldn't picture Dodge using a holiday card as a sample. "Dodge said he'd do an original design instead, and then they could decide if Sammy really wanted it done. When they came back the next day, Dodge handed Sammy a drawing of a classic gothic angel. He worked every detail from the tendrils of the angel's hair caught in the wind to the lacy feathers on her wings." Charlie's fingers fluttered in front of his face. "Sammy had anticipated something small that would cover a fraction of his right shoulder, but Dodge's artwork was a full sleeve. It would take many sessions to complete and a number of days working odd jobs to pay for it, but Sammy and his mother knew it was the perfect design."

"Are they always so elaborate?" Sawyer took a peek at the tentacle that wrapped around Charlie's arm.

"No, some are simple. Dodge's wife only has a lotus flower on the back of her hand. It honors her yoga mentor who died of infection while on vacation in India."

"Wow, that's so sad!" Sawyer sat back in the seat and sighed.

"It's all done in peach and rose colors. There's no black in the design." Charlie waved his hand back and forth. "Most people don't notice it at all." Grady thought he was motioning him to turn and put on his blinker.

Charlie flushed. "No Grady, straight, don't turn!"

Sawyer leaned forward again and asked, "Do girls get big tattoos too?" Charlie's eyes lit up. "Oh yeah, Dodge's friend Amy would go on and on about Alice's Adventures in Wonderland. She asked Dodge if he would do a scene from the book on her back. It was a big commitment." Charlie remembered the months she endured staying out of the ocean while each stage of the tattoo healed. "Dodge spent over a year on a forest that goes from her shoulders to her waist. The Cheshire cat lounges in a tree looking down on Alice, the Mad Hatter, the March Hare, and of course the nasty Queen of Hearts."

"How did she deal with the pain?" Grady grimaced. "The sessions took an hour each. No drugs, no alcohol, no pills. The pain is part of the experience." Charlie wanted Grady to know how ethical tattooing was done.

Grady thought back to the night he got his. Too many beers clouded his judgment. He didn't treat the process with the respect it deserved, and now he was paying the consequences. Grady pulled into Charlie's driveway and braked a little too hard on the gravel. "Thank you so much, Charlie. I have a lot of thinking to do, but at least now I know what my choices are."

Charlie climbed out of the car on unsteady legs, relieved that the wild ride with this teenage driver was over.

"Come by the house Saturday at noon and bring your folks. You can follow us over to Dodge's house in Kailua and you'll get to see how we celebrate a baby's first birthday. Not so long ago it was common for babies to die before they reached a year. It's unusual now, but we've kept the tradition of having a real celebration on the first birthday with friends and family. We make it a true Hawaiian luau."

Charlie waved good-bye. "Aloha. See you Saturday." Sawyer moved to the front seat and together she and Grady drove back to the base, each replaying the events of the morning and attempting to put them into perspective.

"Are you going to tell your dad about today?" Sawyer asked.

"Well, they both wanted to be involved, so I guess I'd better fill them in." Grady replied.

"They'll be excited about the party. It'll be a way for them to meet new people too. It must be hard being isolated on the base with no friends." Sawyer felt sorry for her mom. She knew she was worried that when Bradley left on his mission, she'd have no one to count on besides her and Grady.

"The squadron should have a get-together soon.

They'll want to introduce their new Safety Officer to the troops." Grady said.

"What does a Safety Officer do?"

"The SO makes sure everyone follows procedure so there won't be any accidents. He heads inspections and checks the equipment. Don't worry Slick, the officers' wives will make a point of including your mom in lots of stuff. It just takes a little time."

Sawyer was relieved her mom would have an opportunity to make some new friends, especially people who were experiencing the same problems she was. Bradley's upcoming deployment had them all on edge.

They showed their IDs at the gate and Grady drove past the library. "You think Chloe's working today?" he asked Sawyer.

"I don't know," she shrugged. "Why don't you see if the door's open?"

Grady nodded. "Yep, looks like it," he said, trying to conceal his enthusiasm. "I'll take you home and give Julie the car," he said. "She had errands to do this afternoon. I think I'll ride my bike back here and see if I can talk Chloe into going to lunch with me." Grady smiled as he told her his plan.

Sawyer would rather he spent the afternoon with her, but she nodded in agreement instead. It was useless to compete with Chloe.

CHAPTER 19

The Lunch Date

Grady hoped the long ride from base housing to the library was going to be worth it. When he got to the door, he looked in to find Chloe reaching up to the top shelf of a bookcase, her fingers stretching to grasp a heavy volume that was pushed to the back.

"Let me help you. You don't want that book to fall on your head." Grady grabbed it before it toppled off the shelf.

Chloe gasped. She hadn't heard him come in. She was shocked to see him standing so close that their arms intertwined to catch the falling book.

"Wow, thanks. You startled me." She laughed as he handed her the book.

"I wanted to come and thank you for helping us with the mythology thing." Grady's vocabulary took a plunge in Chloe's presence.

"That's what I'm here for." She grabbed the book to her chest and looked at him through her bangs. "Did you get everything you needed?" She fumbled with a messy stack of papers on the desk.

"We're still working on it, but the printout was enlightening." He shuffled from one foot to the other and clasped his hands behind his back to keep them from shaking. "I, uh, I was, I mean – I was hoping I could take you to lunch," he stuttered.

Chloe looked at the clock. She wasn't supposed to leave the library until closing, but Grady was awfully cute with his shaggy blond hair falling into his eyes. She bit her lip and looked to the ceiling. Grady was afraid she was trying to come up with an excuse not to go, but he tried not to show it.

"Well," she sighed, "I have to stay until 3:00, but maybe you could go to the Package Store and get us some deli sandwiches? I'll clear off the table and we can eat here." Chloe grabbed the stack of papers and shoved them into the bookshelf behind the table.

"Sounds great. Let me take your order." Grady picked up a message pad and pen.

"Chicken, beef, or veggie?"

"Hmm, chicken on wheat." Chloe chuckled as he scribbled down what she wanted.

"Do you like mustard or mayo?" Grady beamed. "Mustard. And don't forget some pepperoncinis!"

Chloe turned to finish clearing the table and hide her blushing face.

"I'll do my best. Be back in a jif." Grady headed for the door with a big grin on his face. He jogged across the street, feeling better than he had in a long time. The deli line was long and it took forever to get the sandwiches made. Grady paced back and forth, impatient for his number to be called. He picked out chips and macadamia nut cookies for dessert.

By the time he got back, Chloe had moved the table to the open doorway to catch the breeze. Grady laid out the picnic while Chloe checked out a book to the only kid to show up all day.

"Is it always this quiet?" Grady asked.

"We don't have many students during the summer, but on Tuesdays I have a reading hour. It's full of little kids. I love doing different voices when I tell them stories. They get so excited." She broke into an unintentional smile, and Grady couldn't help but smile back. He could tell she had a great connection with them. They pulled up two chairs and sat down to their lunch.

"Looks good. I love macadamia nut cookies." Chloe looked up at him as she sipped her soda. Her freckled nose quivered as bubbles escaped from her drink. Grady tried to keep from staring and forced himself to take a bite of his sandwich. "Will you be going away to college in the fall?" he asked.

"Only if I get a scholarship to one of the Mainland schools. We can't afford out-of-state tuition on my dad's military salary. If not, then I'll stay here and go to the U.H. How about you?" She popped a pepper in her mouth and reached for her drink to wash it down.

"I haven't decided yet." Grady eyes narrowed. He didn't want to go into the embarrassing details of his uncertain plans.

"How long will your dad be stationed here?" Grady knew he had to keep the conversation going, but he was running out of topics already.

"At least three years, maybe four. He's up for shore duty in D.C. next." Chloe wiped some mustard from her mouth and hoped she didn't have more lurking on her chin.

"My dad just did D.C." Grady remembered the public school where most of the dependents went. It had some serious problems. "It's a good thing you'll be away at college or out of school by the time you go."

Chloe crunched a potato chip and licked the salt from her fingers, then caught herself and tucked her hands into a napkin. She looked at Grady, but he just glanced away at the clock on the wall, pretending not to see it. She blushed and shook her head with a sigh.

"I think all the history there is cool," she said. "I've always wanted to see the Space Museum and the White House."

Grady was stumped. Historical buildings or museums didn't interest him much. An awkward silence seemed to go on forever and still he couldn't think of what to say next. Picking at his chips, he was relieved when finally Chloe said, "It gets lonely going from place to place, doesn't it?" She bit into her cookie and savored the sweetness. "I'm lucky this is my last fulltime duty station. It's been tough on my mom, too. Dad's deployment to Iraq got extended twice when things heated up over there. We worry about him every day."

Grady felt a lump growing in his throat. "My mom couldn't handle the moves or the deployments. She left a couple of years ago." Grady crumbled his cookie between his fingers. He was surprised he'd shared something so personal. Chloe's eyes welled up with tears.

"I would just die if something bad happened to my dad, but I'm also proud of him for serving our country and taking the risks he does to help keep us safe."

Without thinking, Grady touched his thumb to her cheek to catch a tear. "My dad and I have our differences, but I feel the same way." Grady dropped his hand and held hers for a moment. They could hear a formation of jets flying overhead and waited for the noise to die down.

"Military life is hard on families," Chloe said. She squeezed his hand.

"Yeah, it's hard," Grady agreed. He squeezed back. Not knowing what to do next, he squeezed once more then gathered the sandwich wrappings, the potato chip bags and the cups and took them to the trashcan.

Chloe's heart pulsed. She prepared to close up while Grady moved the table and the chairs back where they belonged. His throat felt dry. "Do you want to go to the beach when you're done here?" he asked.

Chloe thought for a moment and then gave him a warm smile. She looked at him with new appreciation. "Sure, why not?" she said.

Grady helped her finish, and at 3:00 PM sharp she locked the door, and they walked down to the beach. Chloe pulled a beach towel out of her bag, spread it on the hot sand, and they sat looking at the surfers who sat patiently astride their boards waiting for a good set of waves.

"Can you get the sunscreen for me?" Chloe asked, pulling on a straw hat. Grady turned to get the tube and Chloe caught a glimpse of Grady's tattoo.

"That's some tattoo you've got. It looks new and raw. Are you sure you can expose it to the sun?" Chloe's lips were tight as she zeroed in on the tattoo.

Grady didn't know what to say. His face turned red and he turned away. When he felt he'd composed himself, he turned back and said, "I got it on my road trip. Turns out the characters tell the story of a Japanese god named Susanoo. That's why Sawyer and I came to the library. We wanted to research the myth." Grady hoped his simple answer would satisfy her.

While Chloe took in the tattoo, the wind swelled, the sky turned dark and a deluge drenched them. They hurried to gather their things and look for shelter. Grady put his arm around her and they lifted the beach towel over their heads. They huddled together as the rain continued to fall. Then, typical of a Hawaiian storm, the rain stopped and the sun peeked through the clouds.

"That was quite a blessing." Chloe's straw hat drooped and rain dripped off her shoulders. She looked to the East where more clouds were forming and said, "I guess I better make a dash for home." She sounded disappointed. "I'll see you later Grady. Thanks for lunch." Chloe waved as she ran toward base housing.

Grady shook his head. "Some blessing," he muttered.

123

CHAPTER 20

The Consultation

By the time Grady got home the sun was shining and his wet clothes had dried. Julie and Sawyer were in the kitchen cooking up some dish and hustled him out before he could get a glimpse of what was in the frying pan. He joined his dad at the picnic table and began to tell him about the visit to Koi Tattoo.

"It was so clean and professional, Dad. Dodge said that Hawaii has strict sanitation standards. They inspect tattoo businesses on a regular basis. California doesn't have as many regulations, so places like Double Dagger can slip through the cracks." Grady sounded a little disappointed. "Dodge had to take a licensing exam to prove he knew how to protect the clients and himself from AIDS and other diseases. They only give it twice a year, and he had to take it the morning of his wedding. Can you imagine how that must have been?"

Bradley smiled, remembering his own wedding day.

He couldn't fathom trying to focus on a test if he knew he'd be walking down the aisle that afternoon. He shook his head. "Two life changers in one day. I don't think I could do it."

Julie came in balancing a tray over her head. Sawyer stood behind her with the drinks. "Here's our surprise pūpūs!" she announced.

Sawyer laughed as Julie set down the drinks. "That word just cracks me up." Grady tried to keep a straight face and glanced over at his dad. Bradley had his hand over his mouth to hide his smile, and Grady had to laugh.

"Well, we are in Hawaii and we must assimilate." Julie was using her teaching voice again. "But I'll admit, pūpū is pretty funny."

Grady's mouth watered when Julie put down the surprise dish – a steaming plate of Gran's famous buffalo wings. He reached for one, held it high, and said, "Here's to Gran's fine cooking!" He looked at Sawyer and Julie and saw the same look Chloe had when they talked about missing their dads. "It must be so hard for both of you. I know how much you miss Gran, Papa, and Colby too."

Julie's eyes blurred. She put her arm around Sawyer and nodded in agreement. Sawyer hugged her mom back, wishing her grandparents were sitting with them, sharing the buffalo wings and enjoying the beautiful view of the ocean. Then she brought herself back to the present, sat down, took a big gulp of pineapple juice and reminded them, "They'll be here for Christmas. I can hardly wait."

Julie's emotions steadied, and she changed the topic. "Grady, did you decide what you're going to do about your tattoo?"

"Not exactly, but I'd like to borrow the car and go back to Koi tomorrow and talk with Dodge some more. He said it was important for him to get to know me better before he agreed to do anything."

"I think that's a good idea. What's your schedule look like?" Bradley deferred to Julie.

"Sawyer and I didn't find a birthday present for Peggy at the Exchange, so I thought we'd go to Kailua and shop tomorrow." She pulled her hair back and started to pleat it into a nervous braid. She was trying to figure out how to get everybody where they needed to be.

Sawyer nodded. She was excited to be included on this shopping spree. Little girl's clothes were so adorable and so far she hadn't had any opportunity to explore Kailua.

"We could drop you at the tattoo studio and catch up after lunch," Julie suggested.

"Let me call Dodge and see if that works." Grady was touched by Julie's concern. He couldn't see her as his mom, but he knew she cared about him, and he had to admit it felt pretty good. He pulled out his cell phone and the card with Dodge's number on it.

After a short conversation, Grady nodded and said, "Cool, I'll see you at noon." His face relaxed as he looked back at his family. "Done."

The next day Julie followed Grady's direction to Koi Tattoo. She had no idea what to expect, but she was pleased when they parked in front of the studio. Looking through the windshield at the large picture window, she could see the reception area, the counter with the dragon mural behind, and some of the artwork that covered the walls. It looked more like an upscale hair salon than any tattoo parlor she had imagined.

"Bye Julie, and thanks for bringing me, and for helping me make lunch." He grabbed the cooler. "I'll see you guys in a couple of hours." Grady ruffled Sawyer's hair and laughed when she gave him a nasty look.

He found Dodge, head bent close to the mural, painting purple shadows on the dragon's underbelly. Grady watched his purposeful strokes on each scale. Dodge acknowledged him with a wave of his brush. "I always find something else to add when I do a mural like this," he sighed. "In a couple of months I'll be tired of it, paint the whole thing out white, and start a new project with a completely different subject."

He pointed to the sofa. "Have a seat. I'll clean up this brush and be right back."

Grady was too nervous to sit, so he walked around the room, getting a closer look at the artwork on display. He stopped at a painting of an ape looking at a city skyline at sunset. One leafless tree grew between skyscrapers.

Dodge returned. "He's wondering what happened to his world," he said.

Grady felt the ape's isolation. He knew what it felt like to live in someone else's world. "Were you always an artist?" he asked.

"Yeah, as long as I can remember," Dodge said. "My grandmother was my first teacher. She would sit with me for hours explaining the proportions of the body, teaching me perspective, color theory and how to shade." Dodge smiled at the memory. "She always encouraged me and believed in my talent, especially when my parents pressured me to do better in school and have a more practical career."

"I was lousy in school," Grady agreed. "My dad and I have a lot of those talks too."

"How many times have you moved?" Dodge knew how hard it was to start over. He'd left everything to come to Hawaii.

"Six that I can remember. The last was D.C. I never settled in there. The kids were tough on newcomers and I just couldn't make the effort again." Grady sighed.

"Bet you're glad that's over. So what's next?" Dodge asked.

"I don't know. I can't imagine myself going back to school. Academics just don't do it for me. Dad talks about going into the military, but I sure don't want that for a career. I couldn't put my family through it." Grady took a frustrated breath. "Guess I need to get a job somewhere."

"Do you want to stay on the island?" Dodge probed.

"Yeah, I'm just getting used to this family and I don't want to leave them. Not yet."

"Lots of changes there too," Dodge said. He sprinkled fish food into the fish tank and they watched the feeding frenzy. "How's that going?" he asked.

"Better than I thought it would." Grady leaned against the counter and ran his hand through his hair, pushing the long strands out of his eyes. "Julie's cool," he said. "She tries so hard to make things good for all of us. I can tell she and Dad are happy together, but I'm worried about what will happen when he deploys. My mom couldn't take it. I hope Julie can." Grady was unsure.

"And Sawyer?" Dodge asked.

"Ah, Sawyer," Grady shook his head. "I never thought about what a little sister would be like. She's tough, stubborn and loyal. Without her beside me, I don't know how I could have handled all that's happened." He stopped for a moment and imagined not having Sawyer in his life. "I'm a lucky guy."

Grady needed to change the subject before he got too emotional. "How did you decide to become a tattoo artist?"

"I experimented with oils, sculpture, graphic design, pen and ink, all sorts of mediums. I even had an art gallery with a couple of friends, but we couldn't make enough profit to support the three of us." He was picturing their cramped living quarters in the basement of the gallery and the roof vegetable garden that consisted of 3 potted tomato plants. "We had an exhibit featuring the sculptures and paintings of local tattoo masters, but we also had each of them bring a client they'd tattooed to the reception. Hearing the stories behind their tattoos inspired me, so I decided to become a tattoo artist. It was hard to qualify for an apprenticeship. The finest masters only take one student every few years. During those first months, I worked scrubbing floors, sterilizing needles, tracing images, sometimes fourteen hours a day. Most nights I slept on the couch at the studio. It took years of hard work, but now I have my own business, my partner Gina, and I can support a family doing what I love."

"You have a partner?" Grady was surprised.

Dodge nodded, "She specializes in tribal tattoos with characters similar to those on your leg. I'd have her take a look at yours, but she's on the mainland right now."

Grady just shook his head. "Do you sell some of these paintings too?" He was amazed by all the different kinds of art Dodge created.

"I exhibit in Kailua and Honolulu galleries. I do some commission work too, like the painting of Jasmine at Charlie's house." Grady remembered the woman on the beach hanging in the living room.

"It's a beautiful piece. I didn't realize it was Jasmine, but of course that makes perfect sense."

"I only paint subjects that have a message. If someone is moved by a piece, I'll sell it or make a trade for something for the family." Dodge laughed again, "That's how we got our first car. It had plenty of rust, but it was what we needed at the time."

"You ready for lunch?" Grady asked. He pulled a cooler from under the counter. "I made us a couple of seared Ahi salads. Charlie caught the fish this morning."

Dodge looked impressed. He grabbed two bottles of water out of the fridge and they started eating. After a few bites, Dodge said, "So have you've made some progress with figuring things out."

"I guess, but I have a long way to go."

"I like to set just a few goals for myself and focus all my effort on accomplishing them. You might want to give it a try," Dodge suggested.

Grady chewed and thought about it. Then in a calm voice he said, "I want to be a better person for my family, you know, help them like they've been supporting me." Grady paused then added, "But I want to be independent too. I need to get a job and pay my own way. Whatever I do with my tattoo will be expensive, and it's my responsibility to pay for it."

"That's a good start." Dodge nodded.

"I want you to help me with this tattoo." Grady asked.

"What do you have in mind?" Dodge said.

Grady swallowed the last of his water. He began to explain his plan, and a cautious smile spread across Dodge's face.

CHAPTER 21

Peggy's Luau

Sawyer was excited about the luau. She dressed in the aloha shirt her mom bought on their shopping spree to Kailua. It was red with white hibiscus flowers strewn over the shoulders like a lei. Julie and Bradley were glad to be included. They were impressed when Grady told them about his consultation with Dodge, and they were eager to meet him and his family in person. They knew it was important to get to know Charlie and Jasmine too, since Sawyer and Kaleʻa were forming such a strong friendship. Making connections in a new duty station was always difficult. Bradley wanted to make it as easy as possible. His new family had sacrificed so much to follow him here, and he admitted that this move was more difficult. His squadron was scheduled for a long and dangerous deployment in the Middle East. He finally confided his concerns to Julie the night of Kale'a's party. Though she tried to be sympathetic, she was hurt that he didn't feel he could tell her as soon as he found out. He knew he had to work at being more open with his new family, even when the news was bad. Avoiding the deployment or other assignments to come was impossible. Julie encouraged him to spend more time with each of them when he could. The stronger their relationship, the more understanding and supportive they would all be when he left.

A little before noon, they pulled into Kale'a's driveway. Charlie and Jasmine insisted they come in for passionfruit smoothies before going on to the luau. Jasmine shared some of their art with a mix of pride and pleasure. Julie admired the painting of Jasmine that Dodge had done, as well as the dragon he sculpted for Charlie. The painting of the koi was a gift from Sammy's family for Charlie's birthday. He explained that koi eventually turn into dragons and are revered by many islanders.

They found their way out to the lānai and looked out over the bay while they finished their drinks. Julie could see the Marine base shimmering in the distance. The two worlds seemed so far apart. Here they were, chatting with this traditional Hawaiian family, but after the party was over they'd go back to military life on base. She hoped some kind of balance between the two would help Sawyer embrace her new home and that she would focus on the opportunities it provided.

Sawyer kept an eye out for Kanoa. When he wandered out on the lānai she marched over and smiled. "Hi Kanoa, it's great to see you again! Are you joining us at the birthday party?" she asked.

"They're not my kind of people," Kanoa snapped. "Too bad. We brought some great pūpūs. Would you like me to leave some here for you?" Sawyer gave her best smile.

"Don't bother." Kanoa backed away. He gave her the once-over with narrowed eyes, then turned and left.

"Really Sawyer, you don't have to be nice to my brother. He doesn't deserve it. Just ignore him." Kaleʻa was embarrassed.

Sawyer nodded, but she wondered if there might be some way to win him over.

With Charlie in the lead, they caravanned to Dodge's house. Loaded down with pūpūs, they walked up the steps and added their slippers to the pile at the entrance. The double doors were wide open and laughter echoed down the hallway. The party was going strong out back. Sawyer had never seen so many little kids. Tribes of them were running around with rainbow-colored butterfly wings attached to their flapping arms. A small group of boys were driving their toy trucks in the huge sand box. Others climbed up the ladder to the tree house that was perched in a majestic liche tree. Moms and Dads watched on the sidelines, laughing at the scene and interfering only when they needed to.

Sawyer turned to Kaleʻa and asked if they were all somehow related.

"Why?" asked Kaleʻa in surprise?

"The kids are calling all the adults auntie or uncle!" Sawyer exclaimed.

Kaleʻa laughed, "That's the Hawaiian way. Families find friends they can trust. You know, moms and dads who treat their kids like they do. The group becomes one extended family, and all the adults are your aunties and uncles. If a kid needs help riding a bike, skins a knee, or has a special treasure to share, they don't have to look for their parents. Any auntie or uncle will do."

Dodge was showing a small group of guys a new solar oven he built out of metal and mirrors when he caught Bradley's eye. He excused himself and headed over to meet the family. Dodge had a good grip, piercing eyes, a great smile, and a body covered in tattoos.

Bradley was curious about the variety of interlocking images that encircled his arms. The dragon's tail twisted in green vines and was beautifully detailed. Each scale shaded to a florescent glow, but much to Bradley's frustration the body and head were hidden by a tank top advertising Koi Tattoo. He could tell Dodge put a lot of thought into his work, and he wanted to see the whole picture.

"Aloha! I'm glad you guys could come and meet some new friends. There are a few other military families coming too. I'll introduce you when they get here." Dodge turned to look at his daughter and pointed out the chubby birthday girl to her guests.

"That's my daughter Peggy over there with the lei. I think she might eat it before the party is over."

They looked over at a flowered quilt where Peggy sat with her sister Pippy and two other toddlers pulling at the lei around her neck. Just as she began to topple over, an older girl caught her. Grady squinted. Is that who he thought it was? He recognized her long blonde ponytail peeking out from the back of her ball cap. Grady smiled and excused himself from the group with a quick wave as he headed over to the quilt.

"Hey, Chloe. I didn't expect to see you here today." Chloe tilted her head up to look at him and the corners of her lips turned up in surprise.

"Hi Grady! I didn't know you were friends with Dodge."

"I went to talk to him about the tattoo."

"Good idea. Was Dodge familiar with that Susanoo character?"

"Yeah, we had a good talk. How do you know him?" Grady asked.

"When my dad's squadron was being deployed to the Middle East, they all went to Dodge to have their squadron emblem tattooed on their arms. Peggy's picture is in the shop, my dad saw it, and he volunteered me to babysit. I just love her."

"So now you're one of the aunties?" He grabbed the brim of her baseball cap and lifted it to see her face better. She raised an eyebrow and laughed.

"You bet, Auntie Chloe. That's me. What are you doing with my hat, Grady?" She pulled the brim back with a coy look.

Grady shrugged just as a rough-looking guy strutted up and gave Grady a hard look. He wore a tight white tank top to show off his muscles, and it looked like he was trying to grow a beard. Grady thought it wasn't going so well. The dark whiskered patches didn't fill in around his cheeks. His eyes were set a little too close on his face, and his brows were extra thick.

"Jed, this is Grady. His dad just transferred here, too," Chloe said. Grady looked to her for a clue. He figured she was trying to be friendly to a newcomer, which was admirable. He was a newcomer too, but Jed seemed like a handful.

"Hey Grady," Jed said. "Quite a party for a kid's birthday isn't it? No one ever threw me a party like this when I was a kid."

He hiked up his baggy trunks to keep them from sinking too low and shot a sly look at Chloe. She didn't catch it. She was reaching out to Peggy, helping her stand and take a few unsteady steps.

"I'm going to check out the horseshoes," Jed grumbled. "Come on." He gestured Grady to follow him and walked off. Grady shrugged at Chloe and Chloe shrugged back. She turned her attention to Peggy and Grady followed Jed to the side yard. He wasn't sure about Jed, but he was sure he didn't want to leave Chloe alone with him.

CHAPTER 22

Kaleʻaʻs Hula

Sawyer couldn't believe that everyone ditched her! Obviously, Grady was more interested in Chloe than he was in her. Kaleʻa had wandered over to the tree house to boost Pippy up the ladder. Even Julie and Bradley left her to go check out the pit where they'd cooked the pig all night. She followed and stood behind them as Dodge explained how they dug the hole, lined it with lava stones, and set a kiave wood fire. He poked the smoldering pit with a tree branch and explained that when the fire died, they added pork roasts wrapped in foil, and then covered it all with banana leaves, wet burlap sacks, and dirt to seal the underground oven called an imu. The aroma carried on the breeze made her mouth water.

Sawyer wandered back to the lānai, leaned on a post, and watched Dodge's friends chat and laugh and eat in small groups. No one seemed to notice her standing alone. Just as she was really beginning to feel sorry for herself, she felt a hand tap her shoulder. She turned around and saw Dodge's wife, Becka. She was just a little taller than Sawyer and wore a gauzy white strapless dress to show off her golden tan. Her green eyes shone and her smile was open and warm. Sawyer was taken by surprise as Becka crushed her in a bear hug and introduced herself.

"Hi, you must be Sawyer! I'm Dodge's wife Becka," she said. "I was wondering if you could give me a hand? I want to get the cake ready and light the candles. I could use some help with plates and forks, even though the keiki will probably just pick up the cake with their hands."

Sawyer thought hard. She remembered Charlie using that word to describe himself when he was with his great-grandfather. "What are keiki?" she asked.

"Oh, sorry! That's Hawaiian for kids."

Sawyer nodded. That made perfect sense. She jumped at the chance to help and followed Becka into the kitchen. She took one look at the cake and gasped.

"Where did you find this?"

"Dodge and I made it," she said with pride.

The cake was shaped like a butterfly. The wings were decorated like a rainbow, each color blending into the next. Tiny dollops of frosting in alternating blue and purple stars dotted the edge of the cake. The butterfly had big expressive eyes with long lashes and antenna corkscrewed up in the air with sparkling shaves of glittery candy.

"Wow, awesome!" It was all Sawyer could find to say.

"This is what happens when you have an artist in the family," Becka said.

"Did you make the butterfly wings for the keiki to wear too?" Sawyer asked. She was proud to remember another Hawaiian word.

"Yep! That was Dodge's idea too. They make great party favors and the keiki have a great time flying around the yard. Can you take these plates and napkins out to the lānai? As soon as our special performance is over, it's time for the cake."

Sawyer took the supplies and left the kitchen, happy to be needed for such an important mission.

The loud beating of a drum brought everyone together where they were about to be treated to a Polynesian performance. Kaleʻa, dressed in a canary yellow sarong that was bordered by stencils of red sea turtles, came out from behind the drum. She glided barefoot to the center of the lānai wearing a wreath of red hibiscus flowers in her hair and a matching lei that reached to her waist. She began to dance the hula, her hips rolling to the rhythm of the drum. Sawyer got Goosebumps watching her move. All the while, Kaleʻa spun four tennis-like balls attached to ropes in all directions. It was like watching someone do tricks with four yo-yos at once.

Sawyer couldn't believe what she was seeing. She found Jasmine and asked her what they were.

"Those are poi balls. It takes a lot of coordination to spin them in different directions without a mistake," Jasmine answered, keeping her eyes on her daughter.

"Kaleʻa is very talented. Each hand creates a different pattern, and you can see sheʻs dancing at the same time." She beamed with pride.

Kaleʻa ended her dance by pointing her toe and dropping her head in a bow, the poi balls hanging loosely in her hands. She glanced up and smiled as she recognized Sawyer. The crowd exploded in hoots of appreciation, then she handed the balls to her father. That was his cue to start up "Somewhere Over the Rainbow." This time Kaleʻa used her hands to tell the story. A hush fell over the audience. Even the keikis, caught in the magic of the hula, sat in silence. A few moms sniffed back tears, and a few dads, too. She waved her arms up and down to show the blue birds flying. Each word was its own movement. Sawyerʻs favorite was when Kaleʻa scooped her hand from the ground up to the sky to represent a rainbow. The music ended and Kaleʻa bowed once again. The audience burst into applause and surrounded Kaleʻa.

Jasmine rested her hands on Sawyerʻs shoulders. "She did it!" Jasmine whispered. Sawyer could see the sparkle of a tear in the corner of her eye.

"That was so awesome," Sawyer said. She couldnʻt help wondering how it would feel to move like that. "Do you dance too?"

"I started when I was a kid. I remember watching my Grammy dance at The Cove on the North Shore. All the people would stop eating and the restaurant would go silent. The applause was enough to shatter your eardrums."

"Is it just for Hawaiians?" Sawyer asked.

"Of course not," Jasmine gave Sawyer a pat on the head. "In fact, dancing would be a great way for you to learn more about our customs and meet new friends. If you'd like, I can talk to your mother about taking lessons from Auntie Makani. She's a kumu, wise to the old Hawaiian ways, like a kahuna. She's tough as a drill sergeant, but you'll learn the hula and it's a lot of fun." Sawyer was ecstatic. "Oh Jasmine, that would be great! Thank you – I mean, mahalo, right?" "That's right. Mahalo."

Becka appeared with the butterfly cake. Everyone clapped and sang "Happy Birthday" as Dodge carried Peggy up to the cake and had her blow out the single candle. She grabbed a fistful of the butterfly's wing and stuffed it into her mouth. The crowd cheered and made their way to Becka and Sawyer, who cut slices and handed them out. Sawyer looked for Grady, but she couldn't find him. She was surprised he wasn't coming forward. He loved gooey sweets. Chloe was there, so where did Grady go?

CHAPTER 23

Horseshoes

Jed handed Grady the horseshoes and stated, "I'll go first." He tossed his first one into the pit just outside scoring distance and snorted. Grady glanced at him. His reaction was a little much. The second shoe slammed against the backboard, tipped over and looked a lot closer to the stake. Jed snickered and stood back while Grady heaved his shoe high in the air and too far right to count.

"Too bad," Jed said, without meaning it.

Grady ignored him and concentrated on the next throw. It went high and straight, hit the stake and landed just beyond Jed's. They walked to the other end and brushed away some sand. Jed said, "Looks like that's one for me." He worked at keeping a smile from creeping onto his face.

Jed picked up his shoes and aimed. This time his shoe landed with a thud close to the stake. He put more effort into the second one and it slid to the backboard. He turned toward Grady. "You're up," he said. His eyes became slits as he noticed Grady's leg. "Dude, your tattoo looks like the open jaws of a fire-breathing dragon. What does it say?"

Grady debated going into the whole story, but in the end, he just shrugged and said, "It represents the fire inside me." Jed couldn't stop looking at it. "That's so awesome, dude. I want a big tat like that."

Grady just sighed and took his stance. "Have you moved much?" he asked. He was getting pretty tired of talking about his tattoo.

"Yeah, about every two or three years." Jed watched Grady's shoe bang into the stake and slide right. "This is our seventh duty station. It's sure better than the last one in South Carolina. The kids there are so formal, all 'yes ma'am, no sir.' I couldn't stand it. How about you?" Jed's shoulders slumped, and he shook his head as Grady's shoe hit the stake square for a ringer.

"We've been all over too." He pumped his fist as the shoe settled around the stake, "Not much fun sometimes."

The two stood lost in their own experiences. After looking around to make sure no one could hear, Jed took a step closer.

"There's a party tonight on the base, down at the beach by the Hale Koa." Grady looked stumped by the Hawaiian term. "It means the 'Warrior's House,' but in this case, it's the President's guest cottage." Jed liked knowing more than

144

Grady. "It's across the runway out on the point. You'll see a bonfire when you get close.

Some kids that are living on the base and a few locals will be there if we can pull it off. I'm going to convince Chloe to come with me. It'll get pretty wild. It starts at dark and goes late. Stop by if you can get away from the family."

"Sure Jed, thanks, I'll try to make it," Grady said with more enthusiasm than he felt.

The happy birthday song interrupted the game. They watched from the back of the crowd as Peggy blew out her candle and grabbed a chunk of the butterfly cake with her hand.

"Gross!" said Jed. Grady let his smile fade.

"Later, Grady." Jed gave a dismissive wave as he walked off in Chloe's direction. Grady wasn't sure what Jed was up to, but he didn't like it.

The party seemed to be winding down. Sawyer expected to watch Peggy open the pile of gifts that had been put in the living room, but was surprised to discover that the custom was to wait until everyone had left. Becka told her that she would take a picture of Peggy as she opened each present and send it with a thank you note. Not a bad idea. Peggy already felt overwhelmed by the friends, the cake, and the chaos of the party. She tottered over to her mother and pulled at the hem of her dress. Becka picked her up and was rewarded with a smear of chocolate across her cheek. "Yummy," she sighed. Peggy laughed and lunged forward for another swipe at her mother. When Becka took her hand, she cried out and squirmed to get down. Becka looked at Dodge and said, "It's going to be a long evening until her sugar high wears off." He nodded in agreement thinking it was all worth it. The party had been a great success.

Sawyer stood watching as the families said their goodbyes. Grady made his way to her. "Have you seen Chloe?"

"She left with that guy from the base. I think his name was Jed." As soon as she said it, she knew that Grady didn't like it. "He's kind of creepy, don't you think?"

Grady frowned. "I don't trust him, especially with Chloe." Grady knew that they were on their way to the party and it made his stomach churn. "Where are Dad and Julie? I'm ready to get out of here."

"They're saying goodbye to Dodge and Becka," Sawyer answered. "Mom said to meet them in the front yard in a couple of minutes. Did you have a good time?" Sawyer grinned as she bent down to find her slippers in the pile by the front door.

"It's sure different." Grady looked at all the black slippers, trying to figure out which ones were his. "All their friends are so involved with each other, the way really good friends can be, even though some are new to Hawaii and the rest grew up here." Grady paused to think. "Everyone's accepted. I like that."

Sawyer chattered on. "Becka was so nice to me. Did you know that she's a yoga teacher?" Grady wasn't surprised by anything at this point. "She invited mom and me to sunrise yoga on the beach. Grady chuckled at the vision of Sawyer and Julie in one of those strange yoga poses. "I loved the hula that Kaleʻa did. Jasmine said I could take lessons from someone named Auntie Makani and that it was hard but fun. I would meet lots of girls that way and Kaleʻa's dad asked the soccer coach if I could join the summer league. They're called the Lava Ladies because they're so hot. Could you believe that cake?" Sawyer rambled with as much enthusiasm as she could, but she couldn't dent Grady's serious expression. "What's up Grady? Is something bothering you? Is it your tattoo?"

"I'm not so sure about that guy Jed. He's looking for trouble."

"Are you sure it's not just because he took Chloe with him?"

"Yeah, that too," Grady admitted.

"So are you the trouble he's looking for?" Sawyer gave him a poke in the ribs.

Grady swatted her hand away with a chuckle. "I don't know, Slick." Grady rolled his eyes. "Could be."

CHAPTER 24

The Storm

The sun was setting by the time they reached the house. A bank of angry clouds in the east foretold the coming storm. Grady stood outside, looking up and down the beach from the cliff. He turned around when Sawyer came up all smiles.

"I think I'm finally getting comfortable with the move," Sawyer said. "Kaleʻa introduced me to a couple of girls on the soccer team and we're going to scrimmage tomorrow." Grady's eyes drifted from the house to the beach and then back to Sawyer. "Grady?" she asked. "Are you listening?"

"That's cool," Grady muttered. "I'm going out for a while. Tell Dad I'll be back late. Don't wait up."

"You okay, Grady?" Sawyer frowned.

"Yeah, sure!" There was an edge to Grady's tone that he immediately regretted. "I'm sorry, Slick," he sighed. "I don't want to be a jerk, but I've got a lot on my mind." Grady walked away.

Sawyer felt a knot in her stomach. She didn't dare follow Grady in that sour mood, at least not while he could see her. She knew she couldn't just let him go. That evil tattoo must've been causing him trouble again, and she was determined to help him through it. They were getting so close to a solution that would give Grady his life back. Why was he pulling this disappearing act now?

Sawyer walked to the house and up the steps. She was trying to decide how to tell Bradley and her mom that Grady was gone without them getting upset. She knew how much this stunt would worry them.

Grady biked past the O Club and continued down the hill to the massive runway. There was a green light at the kiosk, which meant there were no planes in the landing pattern. He sped across the asphalt and took the narrow road that led to the cabins. Each one was secluded with its own private beach. They were popular with Marines who couldn't afford to take their families away for vacation but wanted to do something special. He walked his bike down the road to the first cabin and saw two kids playing in the sand. He backed away and continued to the next one. Kayaks and surfboards cluttered the yard, but no people were around. Grady heard music and laughter further up the shoreline. He propped his bike against a rusty chain link fence and hiked until he found the Hale Koa perched out on the Point.

Groups of people lounged around the bonfire or in the water nearby, laughing, bodyboarding, or just wading. Chloe and Jed weren't there. Grady squinted and spied the two of them sitting on the edge of the cliff at the end of the Point. Jed had his arm draped around Chloe's shoulder, and he was whispering something in her ear.

It made Grady's skin crawl. He could see Chloe's unease in the way she leaned away from him. He edged his way around the "Restricted Area" sign that blocked the path, then climbed out on the exposed bluff. He almost reached them when a sharp pain shot up his leg from the center of the tattoo. Grady gasped. Sweat broke out on his forehead as he leaned down and touched it. It ached like a Charlie horse, tight and sore. Grady rubbed the area around it. He took a careful step to test the cramp, stretched his heel down until the pain eased, then pressed on.

"Hey Jed," Grady panted, out of breath from the climb. "Nice view from up here."

"Oh hi, Grady!" Chloe breathed a sigh of relief. "Good to see you."

Jed nodded in Grady's direction with his jaw clenched and his eyes narrow. "You're interrupting a private party," Jed said. "We'll catch you back at the cabin later."

Grady's foot slipped on some loose gravel. His knees buckled and he came down hard on the rock next to Chloe. He brushed the gravel from his hands and pretended not to notice Jed's menacing tone. "Ah, Jed, that's not very friendly. You asked me to come to the party and now you want to ignore me?" He rubbed a spot of blood that oozed from his left knee.

"A time and place for everything, man," Jed sneered. Chloe scooted away from Jed and rested her hand on Grady's. "Don't leave," she whispered. She looked up at Jed and said, "Maybe Grady can give us his opinion on taking risks as a way to prove yourself." She shot another pointed look at Grady, but Jed didn't seem to pick up on her hints. "You know," she went on, "like when you get to a new duty station and want to fit in?" Chloe's eyes pleaded with Grady to join in on the conversation.

"I've had to prove myself a few times over the years. They always try to test you." Grady stared at Jed while he spoke, wondering why they were having this discussion. "Some risks are fair, but some aren't worth it."

Jed curled his lip. "Ah, but the thrill!" He drew out the last word. Jed was strung tight. "Not to mention the rewards." He sounded like a lot of bullies that Grady had come across before.

"I don't know, Jed," Grady said. "Sometimes you get more respect by standing up and saying no." Grady wished he'd done that the night at Double Dagger. "I guess it depends on who you're trying to impress."

Jed sprang to his feet and pulled Chloe up with him.

Grady rose to knees and was about to stand when Jed pointed out at the sea. "Storm's coming on strong now. Look at those clouds!" Jed fake-stumbled and threw his shoulder into Grady, knocking him flat. Grady's head hit hard and blackness threatened to overtake him. Before he could react, Jed grabbed Chloe's wrist and pulled her closer to him.

"You are going to do this Chloe, and I bet when we're done you'll agree it was a great high." Jed's eyes gleamed as he dragged her forward.

Grady's vision was blurred and his head pounded, but he could hear Chloe's feet dragging over the gravel. Chloe clawed at Jed's hand gripping her wrist. She turned back to yell at Grady, but it was too late. "Stop it, Jed! You're hurting me. Wait, please wait!" she begged. "I can't do this."

They reached the very edge of the cliff and her slippers slid on the rocks. She lost her balance and fell toward Jed, who jumped and forced her with him. He whooped in triumph as they plummeted down the sloping embankment, tumbled through the wet sand and landed hard in the water, inches from a jagged slab of lava. A wave crashed over them and they held their breath until it washed away.

"What a rush!" Jed shouted.

Chloe couldn't catch her breath before Jed yanked her up. She staggered after him, trying to resist his grip as he pulled her further into the ocean around the lava outcropping to a secluded cove. Her shirt clung to her body, her shorts were soaked and smeared with sand, and she lost a slipper along the way.

The storm that had been sitting out over the East moved in. Thunder boomed and sheets of rain blurred the horizon. The surf pounded the shore and the wind swept the sand so hard it stung her legs. Jed drew Chloe under the rock ledge, through an opening and into an abandoned shelter. She shivered. Her stomach felt like she'd been punched. Jed grinned as they both collapsed on the sandy floor.

"Now that was a thrill," he yelled above the storm. "I found this place yesterday when I was scouting empty cabins for the party. It's a bunker the military built during World War II as a lookout station. That's the concrete base for a machine gun. I bet those old wooden boxes held ammo. Cool, huh?"

Chloe scrambled back to one side, looking for a way out, but she was trapped between Jed and the concrete wall. She was so angry and scared she couldn't find the words to respond. She fought to keep her cool.

"Come on, Chloe. Imagine being stuck here for hours checking the sky for Japanese planes, radioing in a sighting and then blasting them with machine gun fire." She eased herself onto a log that had been dragged into the back of the bunker. Jed sprawled across the opening, blocking her only escape. "These bunkers are all over the base. They're well hidden and very private." Jed's expression terrified her. She heard the crash of a wave and felt water bubbling over her feet. High tide was coming in, and the bunker wouldn't make a safe shelter in the surge of the storm.

Chloe tried to stand, but the roof was too low, so she crouched down and attempted to make her way to the opening. Jed grabbed her arm and pulled her against him. "Jed, please," she begged, "We've got to get out of here now!" Chloe's body trembled at the thought of drowning. "Jed, come on! Can't you see the surge is making the tide come in much higher and faster than normal?"

Still convinced the shelter would protect them, Jed just smiled and said, "No worries. We'll be okay." His eyes were glued on hers. "The tide will turn, you'll see."

CHAPTER 25

The Rescue

Grady managed to get up on his elbows. He had to wait for his swimming head to clear before he could stand. At last, he took a few cautious steps. He squinted through the falling rain, but he still couldn't see them. He staggered toward the cliff's edge, yelling Chloe's name over and over. When he got there, all he found was her slipper. The oncoming tide covered the beach below. They had to be down there somewhere. Grady retraced his steps, slid off the cliff, made his way to a lower ledge and jumped down to the beach. He timed the waves as he painstakingly made his way along the embankment, calling out Chloe's name, desperate for a response. The water came up to his knees and the undertow pulled him down. He fought it and plowed on. He tried stepping up to the rain-slicked rock face to get a better view, but couldn't get a foothold, so crawled on his belly like a snake. He got up on his knees, then stood with great care, balancing with his arms outstretched and turned his head from the point of the cliff where they'd disappeared to the section of the beach where they must've landed. The storm fed the tide. The waves pounded against the base of cliff, but Grady wouldn't turn back. Chloe's safety was more important than his own. He eased down again into the surf and braced himself against a wave that crashed against his chest.

The storm nearly swallowed the sound of Chloe's screams. Grady tried to figure out where they were coming from when he saw her other slipper floating on the water. He called out her name again and strained to pick up a response. He heard Jed answer back.

"Help! Grady! Under the cliff!" Jed sounded desperate.

Grady wiped away the rain pouring off his face and thought he could make out an opening under the cliff. This had to be it. He couldn't stand upright, so kept crawling as water rushed over him again. The wave receded and he opened his eyes, stinging from salt and sand. He struggled through the opening and discovered them crammed together on a log. Then the next surge hit. Water engulfed the cave and washed over their laps. Frantic, they tried to stand, but had to hunch over to avoid the rough concrete roof of the bunker. Grady grabbed Chloe's arm, but another larger surge knocked them down and his hold broke as their heads went under. When the water eased out again, Grady saw their faces watching the opening, now completely underwater. Gathering all his strength, he stood and lunged forward to try again.

"We have to get down on our knees and crawl to get through the opening." Grady spat out water as he spoke.

"But we'll be underwater!" Chloe shook her head, swinging her ponytail from side to side.

"When the wave rushes out, we'll get a breath. It's the only way."

He got a better grip on her hand and pulled her a little closer to the opening in the lull between the waves. They held their breath and went under again. When the wave subsided, they came up for air. Chloe struggled onto her knees to free herself from the suction of the waves. Just as another onslaught from the angry sea engulfed them, Jed wedged himself behind Chloe and pushed her through the opening. The water rushed back and washed Chloe and Grady out of the bunker. Grady lifted Chloe to her feet.

They inched their way through the wash of the waves and crawled up the lava outcropping to safety. They stood on wobbly legs, gasping and coughing out salt water. When their eyes met, they threw their arms around each other.

Chloe swallowed a sob and pulled back to look at Grady. Her expression said it all. "What about Jed?" she whispered.

Grady stroked her back. He hated to let her go and brave the waves again, but he released her, eased off the rock, took a deep breath, and let the next wave carry him back through the opening of the bunker. Jed sputtered as the water receded and his head emerged from the foaming sea. His eyes were wild with fear. He knew another surge would hit soon, and drag him under for good. Grady reached for Jed's arm. His legs went out from under him and he flipped onto his back as water filled the bunker once more. Grady used all his strength to hold on and helped Jed onto his hands and knees.

"When the next one hits and we go under, try to keep the opening in front of you," Grady yelled.

Jed managed to nod before the wave overcame them.

They pressed forward, and when the tide ebbed, it spat them out and set them free. Grady dragged Jed over to the lava rock and helped push him up and out of the churning water. They collapsed beside Chloe and stared back at the bunker, now completely submerged.

Jed shook his head and looked at Chloe. "Sorry," was all he could manage.

Grady glared at him, but he read a look of real remorse on Jed's face. "You're on your own now," Grady said. He put his arm around Chloe. They scooted off the rock into the water and made their way along the embankment to safety.

CHAPTER 26

Sawyer's Escape

Julie greeted Sawyer as she entered the house. "Hey honey, wasn't that fun? Did you have a good time?" She looked around and noticed Grady wasn't with her. "Where's Grady?" she asked.

Sawyer bit her lip and said, "He's gone. I don't know where he is." Bradley strolled in from the kitchen with a cup of coffee and a shocked expression.

"What do you mean he's gone?" Sawyer was convinced they'd get angry and yell at her, but Bradley's voice was soft and purposeful.

"I don't know!" she repeated, frustration coloring her voice. "He just left!"

Bradley set down his mug harder than he intended and splattered hot coffee over his hand. He swore and Julie gave him a warning look. He stared at her with such sadness. Sawyer understood their concern. She was worried too.

"I don't know why he stormed out, but he seemed really upset," she admitted.

Julie and Bradley were at a loss. They sat quietly, tension building, unable to do anything but wait. Sawyer couldn't stand it. She paced in her room but it didn't help. She heard them talking and whispering, then silence. It dawned on her there was one place Grady might have gone. She opened the window, stepped onto the stool Papa built for her, threw one leg over the sill and then the other, and climbed out feeling like a secret agent. The trade winds were blowing and it looked like rain out over the ocean, but it wouldn't take long to go down to the beach. Maybe she could find Grady and convince him to come home.

The wind was howling by the time she reached the steps, the sky a cloud-covered gray. It was useless to try and call out Grady's name. She saw a silhouette down on the rocks and her heart started racing. The closer she got, the more certain she was that it was Grady hunched down at the end of the jetty. Sawyer stepped gingerly on the stones. She was glad she'd put on sneakers instead of slippers. It was dangerous, but she only had a little further to go before she could tell it was him for sure.

CHAPTER 27

The Search

Bradley heard a car drive up and saw headlights shining in the window. The screen door creaked and Bradley rushed over. Chloe and Grady stood in the doorway soaked and covered with sand. "What happened?" Bradley said. "Where in the world have you been?"

Julie swallowed a sob of relief and scrambled to grab some towels. "I'm just so glad you're home safe," she said.

Chloe wrapped the towel around her body and clutched it, shivering. "Jed got me into a lot of trouble.

We got caught in the storm and we almost drowned in a bunker. Her teeth chattered as she spoke. "Grady found us." She looked at him with such tenderness and continued, "He risked his life to save us both." Chloe reach out and took Grady's hand.

He squeezed it and said, "Some kids who were partying in one of the cabins gave us a ride home."

Bradley and Julie looked at each other. It was a lot to take in. In the midst of the chaos, no one noticed that Sawyer hadn't joined them. She must've heard what was going on.

"Where's Sawyer?" Grady asked. "In her room," Bradley said.

Grady jogged down the hall, but when he opened the door and called her name, he was met with an empty room and wind blowing through the open window.

Grady ran back to the living room. "She's gone!" "Gone? Where? How?" Julie shouted.

Grady sighed and stared at the ceiling fan.

"We didn't see her at the party or on the way home, but I know where she goes sometimes when things are tough."

Bradley grabbed a flashlight and they raced to the beach. The rain persisted and the journey was slow and difficult. They stopped at the steps and scanned the beach with the flashlight, but there wasn't enough light to see clearly. The tide splashed against the bottom step. The surf covered the sand and made the rocks treacherous. Julie and Chloe walked down a few steps until their feet were touching the water, but Bradley put up a warning hand and shouted, "It's too dangerous. Stay back!"

Then Bradley and Grady stepped off the last stair and waded through wet sand and the churning sea. The sharp edges of the lava-crusted jetty made it even harder to walk. Bradley pointed the flashlight out toward the end of the jetty again and shot the beam back and forth. The sheets of rain captured the light. They couldn't see further than a few feet.

"Try holding it lower!" Grady yelled. "Follow the rocks out to the end! Maybe we'll catch a glimpse of her along the way!"

The light was dim, but Grady spotted something red within the streaks of gray and black. He grabbed his father's arm. "That's her t-shirt!" Then he saw her. She stood waving her arms at them with water splashing around her ankles and up her legs. Bradley lost his balance and slumped to his knees. He couldn't seem to regain his footing.

"Stay here, Dad," Grady said. "Keep the flashlight steady. I'll go get her."

Bradley nodded and did his best to focus the light on the rocks, awash with foam as the waves continued to cover and expose them. He felt terrified and helpless as he watched his son make each tentative step on the slick wet lava. Grady staggered on a rope of seaweed that covered the sloping outcrop. He blinked his eyes and wiped away the salty water so he could keep Sawyer in his sight. She stood calmly now, confident that Grady would rescue her. When he reached her, he planted his feet, pulled Sawyer into his arms, and held her tight.

"I've got you, sis, I've got you," Grady whispered. "I thought I saw you," she sobbed, "but it was just the shadows on the water. When I finally made my way out here, I realized I was alone and I couldn't get back in." Sawyer shook all over. "The water kept rising and I couldn't see where to step. I panicked. I was so afraid that if I slipped, I'd get washed away with the tide."

Grady held her. "It's okay," he murmured. "We're going back now. Hold on to me and we'll take one step at a time," Grady's voice was gentle but commanding. Sawyer thought he sounded a lot like Bradley. "If you think you're going to fall, clutch my arm tighter, and we'll stop. Ready, Slick? We can do this."

They stood for a long moment, took a deep breath together, and worked their way back to the beach.

Pausing only a few times to regain their balance, they eased off the rocks and Bradley reached out to grab them. Together, they waded through the water toward Chloe and Julie. They climbed the first three submerged steps before Sawyer could let go of Grady and reach for her mother, crying in relief.

"I've never been so terrified in my life!" Julie said. She folded her daughter into a beach towel and wrapped her arms around her. "It was horrible having to see the three people I love most so close to being lost forever, and all I could do was watch." Bradley and Grady joined them in an awkward family hug. Chloe watched and smiled, and together they found their way back home.

CHAPTER 28

Safe and Sound

The house was peaceful. The rain had stopped. Chloe sat in a big chair wearing Julie's t-shirt and shorts, close to sleep. Sawyer was wrapped in her old bathrobe. She clutched Gaboochie and listened to Grady tell Chloe the story of Susanoo and Orochi's battle. Suddenly, Sawyer sat upright and joined in.

"Grady, don't you realize what's happened? You fulfilled the legend. You saved Chloe from Jed. She's the princess and he was the eight-tailed dragon. Maybe the curse is over!"

"I don't know," Grady said. "I don't like Jed, but he's not a monster. He's just a lost kid. The dragon's part of me, too, and I'm going to have to realize when he's rearing one of his eight ugly heads and cut it off." Grady grinned. "Just like my tattoo, it's never going to go away completely, so I'll have to learn how to live with it."

Sawyer ran her thumb back and forth over Gaboochie's ear. It was worn down from years of stroking it when Sawyer needed comfort.

"I'm really sorry I made you risk your life again," she said. "I was so caught up in your problems. I wanted to solve them myself to prove I was good little sister, but I guess I blew it." She tried to keep from crying, but her eyes misted up. Grady reached over and rubbed her head.

"Hey, don't talk like that. You're a great little sister.

You never gave up trying to help me with the mess I made. A guy couldn't hope for a better sister." He gave her an affectionate jab in the arm.

Sawyer was so touched that she gave in to her tears.

Grady brushed them away and stood up. "It's getting late," he said. He glanced over to see Chloe snoring softly. "I've got to take Chloe home and explain what happened to her mom. Dad, can I take the car?" Bradley got up from the couch to grab the keys.

"Of course, Grady," he said. Julie walked over to Chloe and gave her shoulder a little shake. Chloe gasped and opened her eyes, unsure of where she was, but she smiled when she saw Julie standing over her.

"I'm so relieved you're safe," Julie said. "Take care. I'll give your mom a call and we'll plan a get together soon."

A look of relief spread over Chloe's face. "That would be great! She's pretty lonely right now, and I know she'd appreciate it."

Julie leaned down to give her a hug. Chloe closed her eyes to absorb Julie's warmth, then pulled back and said, "I'll wash these clothes you let me borrow and get them back to you by the end of the week."

Julie shook her head. "No worries," she said. "Any time."

Grady held out his hand and Chloe grabbed it to pull herself off the couch with a yawn. Julie gave her a pat on the back as they turned to go.

Then he bent down and gave Sawyer a poke in the nose. "When I get back, I'm gonna nail that damn window shut," he said.

Sawyer chuckled. "You really think that's gonna make a difference?" Grady threw his hands up in the air and they both laughed as he walked out the door with Chloe.

The trade winds blew soft and warm as Grady and Chloe looked down at the sea below. The tide was low and the crescent moon shined through the last of the storm clouds. The water sparkled as it slapped against the jetty. Chloe stopped and tugged on Grady's hand to turn him towards her. She stood on tiptoes and kissed him. Grady leaned in, closed his eyes, and accepted the kiss. He could tell it was more than a 'thank you'. His romantic side took over and he let himself believe it was the first of many to come. They pulled back to take a look at each other's faces. Chloe had a mischievous look on her face. "Again," she demanded, and yanked on his shirt to pull him into another kiss. Grady's lips closed over hers and for the first time in ages, he felt like he was where he belonged.

CHAPTER 29

The New Tattoo

It had been a month since the storm. Dodge and Grady had been meeting to discuss the design almost every day. They'd pored over kanji, talked with a Japanese scholar that Jasmine recommended, and made sure the new tattoo would honor the old traditions.

Grady had the offending middle characters removed, and now that area had healed. He was ready for Dodge to rework and complete the tattoo.

He watched Dodge shave his leg and wipe it down with antiseptic. The tattoo machine hummed as Dodge dipped the needles in the ink. He pressed just enough to pierce Grady's skin. Grady thought he knew what to expect, but he winced anyway. The burning pain was part of the experience, but it couldn't compare to the nightmares.

Grady tried to focus on anything else. He thought of Chloe waiting for him at the soccer game.

She'd offered to come with him, and in one way he wanted her to, but this was between him, Dodge, and the dragon. He closed his eyes. He thought about his mother leaving them. That hurt a lot more than the needles. He hoped she was happy in her new life. He realized his mother had given all the love she was capable of, and it wasn't fair to judge her. He tried to recall all of the duty stations he'd lived in, and name the friends from each one. He had to admit that there were always a few. He wished he could go back in time and try harder. He thought about his new life and his new family.

"Okay, Grady. I'm done for now." Dodge's voice brought him back to reality.

Grady took the mirror Dodge offered. He looked down.

"You were right to remove the silver platter, since you're not royalty, and of course, that noisy crow had to go," Dodge said.

Grady smiled. "Now it means my foundation is respect. It's a lot to live up to, but I'll do my best. You did a great job using the remains of the old characters to create the ying and the yang. Though they are usually thought of as opposites, they do compliment each other and interact to make our world dynamic."

Dodge nodded. "Yeah, I was inspired by Sawyer's idea to add the elements of water, wind, and earth to the flames. They tell a more complete story about life."

"She does have a gift," Grady conceded. "In fact, she wants you to tattoo my other leg with the same themes, but use our family's initials instead of the Japanese characters."

Dodge rubbed the bridge of his nose and shook his head with a nervous laugh, "Not any time soon," he said.

Grady went on despite the warning, "She wants you to leave room for any new family members, too." Dodge laughed. "Is there something I don't know?" Grady shrugged. "I don't know either. Not for sure."

He inspected the new tattoo. It was brand-new, red, and raw, but this was something he wanted on him forever.

Dodge looked into Grady's eyes. "You're different, Grady."

Grady nodded. "Yeah," he said. "I've learned a lot. I don't have the words to tell you how much your support means to me. I'm looking forward to that longboard lesson and the fishing trip. We still on for that?"

"We have plenty of time for all that and more," Dodge smiled. "I may even get you over to dig some furrows and plant some seeds for the fall garden."

"I'm all for it, as long as I can bring Sawyer with me.

Her grandparents made her quite a gardener and chef." Grady shook his head, remembering her chopping carrots with a butcher knife in a silver blur. She wasn't even slowed down by the head of cabbage. A few big whacks and it was cold slaw.

"You better hustle out of here," Dodge said as he pulled off his plastic gloves. "Sawyer will be looking for you at the soccer game." He gave Grady a slap on the back. "Cheer her on for me!"

"Thanks again, Dodge. We'll see you at the barbecue."

Grady hurried out the door and down the street to the schoolyard. Though his leg was tender, he ran across the parking lot and around the fence, in search of girls in red jerseys. He spotted the team going on the field for the final quarter. He joined his dad, Julie, Chloe, and Kaleʻaʻs parents on the sidelines, panting from the run. The Lava Ladies drove the ball up the field, but the Sharks' fullback kicked it back. Grady raised his pant leg and pulled off the cellophane to show his dad the new tattoo. Bradley smiled and motioned for Julie to take a look. She touched Grady's shoulder and kissed him on the cheek. It meant a lot to him. His mom could have her own life, but he was happy to have Julie in his. Chloe bent down and stared at the completed tattoo. She gave Grady her stunning smile and a thumbs up. Charlie and Jasmine took a turn examining it. They nodded their approval and Charlie shook his hand. Then Grady carefully pulled the cellophane over the vaseline-covered artwork and lowered his pant lag. Their attention turned back to the game as the Lava Ladies passed the ball back and forth up the field.

"The coach is one of my fishing buddies," Charlie said. "At the beginning of the season he promised the girls that each one would score a goal. Some of the weaker players never get that opportunity on other teams."

The crowd erupted in whoops and hollers as Sawyer kicked the ball to Kaleʻa. She dribbled it into a perfect position and passed it to Jenna who took two hesitant steps then drilled the ball past the Sharks' goalie and scored the winning goal. The ref blew his whistle three times signaling the end of the game and the teams lined up for high fives. The parents and fans gathered with arms raised high, to form a bridge. A blur of red jerseys ran through it and joined their families in celebration.

"Glad you made it!" Sawyer threw her arms around Grady.

"Good game, Slick. That was a nice assist." Grady gave Sawyer her water bottle and found a towel to wipe the sweat from her forehead.

"How did your tattoo session go? How much did it hurt?" Sawyer was full of questions as usual.

Grady just smiled and shook his head. He was getting used to Sawyer's rapid fire. He pulled up his pant leg to show her the new tattoo. She knelt down, lifted the cellophane, and took in every detail.

"You can barely see where the old crow used to be. I like the way he used the four elements with the ying and yang."

"Of course you do," Grady said. "It was your idea."

Sawyer shrugged. "Guess you can't swim for a while," she said.

"Nope, but it's worth it."

She grabbed his hand and they followed their parents to the car. They were off to the little green market where the team met for the weekly barbecue. As they drove up front, the smell of hamburgers hit their noses. Chloe headed off toward a group of friends and waved for Grady to follow. Bradley and Julie joined Kale'a's parents at one of the benches to talk about Grady's new tattoo. Julie rested her head on Bradley's shoulder. He put his arm around her and pulled her close. "We're a new family, but we've already been through a lot," she said. "It's brought us together."

Jasmine took Julie's hand and they beamed at each other. "Now that Grady's got this tattoo thing behind him, has he given any thought to his future?"

That caught them off-guard. Bradley and Julie paused to share a look, then Bradley cleared his throat and said, "We know he wants to stay here, but no military, and no school. I guess he'll look for a job," he sighed. He was resigned to Grady's decision.

Jasmine poked Charlie in the ribs with her elbow.

He paused for a moment. Then he turned to find Grady talking with his new buddies and waved him over. "Hey!" he shouted. "Come over here for a second." Grady excused himself and made his way to the adults. He worried he'd done something wrong. "You like fishing?" Charlie asked.

"Yeah, sure," Grady said, bewildered.

"I need someone to clean tackle, swab decks, and cut off fish heads," Charlie said. "You interested?" He watched Grady's expression turn from confusion to amazement.

"I'd be honored," Grady said and lunged forward to shake his hand. Charlie took a step back to keep from getting knocked over.

"I'll pick you up at the main gate tomorrow," he said. 2"I'll drive." Charlie snorted as he remembered their last wild ride. "Now get back to that pretty girl before she gets bored." Grady gave him an appreciative slap on the back and headed back to the table. "Oh, Grady!" Charlie added. Grady stopped and turned to face him. "I'll be there at 4 AM. Don't be late." Charlie got a kick out of Grady's crestfallen face.

Grady took a deep breath and yelled back, "Cool. See you then."

Sawyer looked around at her new friends and family.

She was actually beginning to feel at home. Kanoa sat alone at the far table, but even he gave her a nod when she looked his way. Christmas would come in a few short months and she was excited to share her adventures with Gran and Papa. Wait until they saw the waterfalls! She giggled as she thought of them getting caught in a "blessing." Hawaii wasn't Kansas, but whether there were wheat fields or the endless sea, it didn't make much of a difference to her. The important thing was being surrounded by family and friends.

She glanced over to Grady and Chloe. She saw them share a look as Chloe took his hand under the table.

No matter what Grady said about "battling his inner dragon," Sawyer still wanted to believe the myth of Susanoo had been fulfilled. Grady saved Chloe and her. He may not be a god like Susanoo, but he certainly was her super hero.

Grady stole one of Chloe's fries, dipped it into a bowl of ketchup and chomped it down. Chloe gave him a dirty look and a playful slap on the wrist. "What?" he said. "Don't you want to share?" She rolled her eyes.

"Sawyer was great today," Chloe said.

Grady nodded. "Yeah, she's a determined little thing, isn't she. I wish I were as heroic as she is.

Chloe blushed and gave him a peck on the cheek. "That's okay Grady, you're a great sidekick," she said.

Grady laughed, but he had to admit it was true.

GLOSSARY OF HAWAIIAN WORDS AND TERMS

a hui hou kākau (ah hoo wee hoh kah koh) – till we meet again

aloha (ah lo hah) – hello, goodbye, love

ʻaumakua (ah mah koo ah) – family or personal gods, deified ancestors

e komo mai (eh koh moh my ee) – welcome, come in

Hale Koa (hah leh koh ah) – warrior's house

haole (how leh) – foreigner or white person

hula (hoo lah) – a traditional Hawaiian dance

kahuna (kah hoo nah) – priest

keiki (kay kee) – child or children

kumu (koo moo) – a teacher

lānai (lah ny ee) – deck or patio

lei (ley) – a flower garland

lōlō (loh-loh) – crazy

mahalo (mah-hah-lo) – thank you

'ohana (O-hah-nah) – family

pau (pow) – finished, done

poi balls (poh ee balls) – balls attached to a cord and spun during a hula performance

pūpū (poo-poo) – appetizer

'ukulele (ooh kah ley lee) – stringed instrument, small guitar

Hawaiian Names

Kaleʻa – Filled with joy

Kanoa – Ordinary person

Kekoa – Courageous

Kōnane – Bright

Lani - Sky

Makani – Strong

ʻOlina - Joyous

Mauananui - Big mountain

DISCUSSION QUESTIONS

Choose a character that faces a problem similar to your own and discuss how to resolve it.

The Sommers face numerous changes as a newly blended military family. Discuss these and how they adjust to living together.

List the references to the color red in the story. What does red symbolize?

Discuss the reasons for wearing slippers and taking them off when entering a Hawaiian home.

How does Grady's life parallel Susanoo's? Where do the similarities end?

Write a myth of your own.

Pick a Hawaiian tradition and explain its origin and importance.

What dragons do you face in your life?

Explain the reasons for Kanoa's strange behavior.

What do you think will happen with Grady and Chloe's relationship in the future?

Give examples that show Sawyer's loyalty and determination.

How has military life affected Grady?

What options were available to Grady concerning his tattoo? Which one would you have chosen?

Though Gaboochi doesn't talk, he has an important role. What is it? Do you have a Gaboochi in your life?

How is Jed's experience with the military similar to Grady's? What are his dragons?

What makes Kalc'a such a great friend?

What challenges will the Sommer's family face in the future?

RESEARCH PROJECTS

What is the importance of sugar plantations in Hawaii?
What is the history of the hula?

What is the importance of King Kamehameha and the Homestead Act of 1848?

How were the Hawaiian Islands geologically created? Are more being formed?

How does the agriculture and food production in Hawaii effect their traditional dishes?

ART AND MUSIC PROJECTS

Draw a picture of one of the character's tattoo.

Draw the images would you choose to represent your journey so far?

Pick a song and create the hand movements for a hula. Draw a picture of Peggy's butterfly cake.

Using tennis balls and string, make poi balls and practice spinning them.

Make a class mural that depicts the Hawaiian sky, land, and sea.

ABOUT THE AUTHOR

Patricia Distad, like many authors, drew inspiration for Island Girl from her own experiences. She married a Navy pilot and taught middle school language arts at the Naval Air Station in Lemoore, California. She supported her students as they dealt with the hardships of having their fathers gone on long deployments and moving to new duty stations that uprooted them from their friends and neighbors. Like most military wives, she experienced the stress of long separations, and concern for her husband's safety as he flew daily training hops as well as combat missions in Vietnam.

Patricia's mom, Peggy, was an artist and shared her passion with her daughter and grandchildren. She mentored her grandson as he struggled in school and encouraged him to explore a career in art. He became a tattoo artist,   moved to Hawaii, married, and has two daughters. They have embraced the culture and take great pleasure in sharing their island life with their friends and family.

Patricia and her husband, John, live in Camarillo and travel frequently to Hawaii to visit. They often stay on Kaneohe Marine Base at the lodge or the cabins, and once spent three nights at the Hale Koa. They play golf there, enjoy the beach, go to the Exchange, and observe the military families who are experiencing many of the same challenges they did while on active duty.

Printed in the United States
By Bookmasters